Of Mice and Men and Zombies: Part One

Ryan Colley

***

Edited by Apollo Editorial Service

https://www.facebook.com/ApolloEditorialService

Cover art by www.fiverr.com/oliviaprodesign

DEDICATION

As always, this is for my mum, sister and partner.

Also for my grandad Pete who helped me proofread my first book, even though he can't stand these grisly tales.

In memory of Grandma Pam Stubbs, who welcomed me into her family and gave me the keys to my freedom.

In memory of Heppy, who was a good dog.

ACKNOWLEDGEMENTS

There are a few people I'd like to thank:

My GCSE English teacher, Mrs Rowe, who encouraged my creative writing and introduced me to Of Mice and Men.

The author of Of Mice and Men, John Steinbeck, who helped influence my writing (beyond this novella) with his amazing works.

And you, the reader.

INTRODUCTION

I remember when I first read Of Mice and Men. It was during my English GCSE's at school and I had to analyse how each character was alone and segregated by their own imperfections – perceived or real. Initially, I thought it was a well-written novella about a subject I cared little about. The more I read the novella, the more I got drawn in. The characters, the era, the setting; it was fantastic and different. However, an aspect that set it above everything else for me was the final chapter. It was tense and emotive. For me, it made the novella impressive. Over a decade later, the ending has stayed with me and still gives me chills when I think about it. I would even say it influenced my own work to some degree. So, naturally, I added zombies.

Why a satirical take on a classic?

Originally I wrote a sequel to the original novella as a joke for friends, which I then turned into a comic for the same friends. That is all it was, a joke. I eventually revisited the idea when I rediscovered the comic when moving. I decided I would make take another crack at making changes to the classic novella years later. This time I was inspired by other mash-up novels combining classics with other contemporary ideas and movie monsters. However, the idea for the Of Mice and Men mash-up was an idea I had many years prior, and seeing the success of these other novels is what gave me the motivation to give it another go.

As a result of these new novels putting twists on older ones, I became a lot more interested in other classic novels and began to read them based on their own merit. I hope that this novella influences others to read the original Of Mice and Men in the same way that other mash-ups influenced me, because it truly is a novella that is worth reading.

What is different?

I have changed a few aspects of the novella, and this not to 'improve' it in any fashion, but ensure that the original novella seamlessly matches with my own style of writing. This includes certain ways speech is written, as well as the general narrative voice. I wanted to keep the novella as true to the themes and ideas as I could whilst also adding my own influence.

Another change is the use of the word "negro" outside of speech. When the novella was written, it was an acceptable term. The use the word "negro" outside of speech was, in my opinion, Steinbeck's way of disassociating himself from the racist language used by the characters. The world has changed since then and the term "negro" is also no longer acceptable. I believe, if Steinbeck was alive today, he would not have used that term when the voice of the writer spoke through the novella. As a result, that term has been changed to something more appropriate for a modern writer's voice. In the words of Steinbeck himself when referring to his background, "I am sad for a time when one must know a man's race before his work can be approved or disapproved".

Why the apocalypse?

The Great Depression, the era of the original novella, was what I believe to be one of the first true human era apocalypses. True, the world didn't end, but neither does the world in most apocalypse fiction. However, during The Great Depression, the world was irredeemably and unequivocally altered and become one which was no longer recognisable. People wandered the great outdoors, never knowing if they would have a home, be able to make a living, nor have food, or even just survive. This apocalypse wasn't brought about by monsters or movie villains, but by man – a trope often found in apocalypse fiction. For me, that is why the setting for Of Mice and Men lends itself so well to the idea of the dead walking – Lennie and George are already surviving in a broken world together, and I am hoping the rewrite I have done will show that. Plus, zombies are what I know best.

For readers of my Among the Dead series, this is a separate world with the undead in it – there is no crossover, although readers will be able to notice references to other zombie fiction that I heavy-handedly put in! This is a standalone series and there will be a sequel … when it's out depends on how well this first one does, then I will rewrite that Of Mice and Men sequel I wrote all those years ago.

Anyway, I hope you enjoy "Of Mice and Men and

Zombies" and please read the original by John Steinbeck. In fact, it's preferable that you read the original novella before this one – you may even enjoy this version of it more if you do!

CHAPTER 1

A few miles south of Soledad, the Salinas River drops in close to the hillside bank and runs deep and green. The water is warm too, for it has slipped twinkling over the bloody yet yellow sands in the sunlight before reaching the narrow pool. On one side of the river, the golden foothill slopes curve up to the strong and rocky Gabilan Mountains, but on the valley side the water is lined with trees – willows fresh and green with every spring, carrying in their lower leaf junctures the debris of the winter's flooding. Decaying bodies with mottled grey flesh and recumbent limbs that lay open palmed towards the sky and buoyant in shallow water, their once-life gone. On the sandy bank under the trees, the leaves lie deep and so crisp that the undead makes a great lumbering as it moves amongst them announcing its movements. Rabbits come out of the brush to sit on the sand in the evening if the area is secure, and the damp flats are covered with the drag marks of the stumbling undead with the frantic footsteps of the living trying to escape them.

There is a path through the willows and among the sycamores, a path is beaten hard by the living running down from the ranches as the land they protected became overrun, and beaten then harder by the creatures which were once human who followed hungrily when the sun was high and visibility worked for them. In front of a low horizontal limb of a giant sycamore there is an ash pile made by many fires of the scared trying to survive a harsh night; the limb worn smooth by men who have sat on it, as well as those who were torn down from it and feasted upon when undead creatures were drawn to the flames as that licked the warm night air and illuminated those trying to hide.

The evening of a hot day started the little wind to moving among the leaves, which shifted the air among the dead; the stench of rot thick on the breeze. On the sand banks the rabbits sat as quietly as little grey sculptured stones, wary that their own movement would attract unnatural predators. Then, from the direction of the state highway, came the sound of able-bodied footsteps on crisp sycamore leaves. The rabbits hurried noiselessly for cover, for any two-legged being were a threat. For a moment the place was lifeless, and then two living men emerged from the path and came into the opening by the green pool.

They had walked in single file down the path, and even in the open one stayed behind the other. Both were dressed in denim trousers and in denim coats with brass buttons. Both wore brown, shapeless hats and both carried tight blanket rolls slung over their shoulders. The first man was small and quick, dark of face, with restless eyes and sharp, strong features. Every part of him was defined: small, strong hands, slender arms, a thin and bony nose; a man who had survived. He had an axe slung over his shoulder, the head often used for cutting more than just tree limbs. On his hip rested a Luger, one which had seen more action than should be allowed. Behind him walked his opposite: a huge man, shapeless of face, with large, pale eyes, and wide, sloping shoulders; he walked heavily, dragging his feet a little, the way the undead struggled to move from under their own weight. His arms did not swing at his sides, but hung loosely.

The first man stopped short in the clearing, and the follower nearly ran over him. He took off his hat and wiped the sweat-band with his forefinger and snapped the moisture off. His huge companion dropped his blankets and flung himself down and drank from the surface of the green pool, and he drank with long gulps, snorting into the water like a horse. The small man stepped nervously beside him.

"Lennie! Lennie, for God sakes, don't drink so much," he said sharply. Lennie continued to snort into the pool, trying without success to stop his thirst. The small man leaned over and shook him by the shoulder and added, "Lennie. You gonna get the Walkin' Plague if you ain't got it already."

Lennie dipped his whole head under, hat and all, and then he sat up on the bank and his hat dripped down on his blue coat and ran down his back.

"That's good," Lennie said breathlessly. "You drink some, George. You take a good big drink."

He smiled happily. George unslung his bindle and dropped it gently on the bank with his axe.

"I ain't sure it's good water," he said. "Looks kinda dirty … like the Sick Ones been in it."

Lennie dabbled his big paw in the water and wiggled his fingers so the water arose in little splashes; rings widened across the pool to the other side and came back again. Lennie watched them go.

"Look, George. Look what I done," he said in amazement. George knelt beside the pool and drank from his hand with quick scoops.

"Tastes all right. Don't really seem to be runnin', though. You never oughta drink water when it ain't runnin', Lennie. And only in small bits," he admitted and explained, then he said hopelessly, "You'd drink out of a gutter if you was thirsty."

He threw a scoop of water into his face and rubbed it about with his hand, under his chin and around the back of his neck. George looked at his hand, seeing that there was blood on it. He knew it wasn't his own, but rather the blood of one of the undead that he felled with his axe a few hours before. Then he replaced his hat, pushed himself back from the river, drew up his knees and embraced them. Lennie, who had been watching, imitated George exactly. He pushed himself back, drew up his knees, embraced them, and looked over to George to see whether he had it just right. He pulled his hat down a little more over his eyes, the way George's hat was. George stared morosely at the water. The rims of his eyes were red with sun glare. There was also darkened bags beneath those eyes – days of exhausting travel and survival ensured that.

He exploded suddenly and angrily, "We could just as well of rode clear to the ranch if that bastard bus driver knew what he was talkin' about. 'Just a little stretch down the highway', he says. 'Just a little stretch.' Goddamn near four miles, that's what it was! Four miles of Sick Ones between there and here! Didn't wanta stop at the ranch gate, that's what! Too goddamn lazy to pull up. Wonder he isn't too damn good to stop in Soledad at all. Kicks us out and says 'Just a little stretch down the road.' I bet it was more than four miles. Damn hot day."

Lennie looked timidly over to him and asked cautiously, "George?"

"Yeah, what you want?" George asked sourly, his eyes flicking to Lennie.

"Where we goin', George?" Lennie asked innocently. The little man jerked down the brim of his hat and scowled over at Lennie.

"So you forgot that already, did you? I gotta tell you again, do I? You're a crazy bastard!" George spouted in frustration.

"I forgot," Lennie said softly. "I tried not to forget. Honest to God I did, George."

"Okay. Okay. I'll tell you again. I ain't got nothin' to do. Might just as well spend all my time tellin' you thin's and then you forget them, and I tell you again," George abated, and sighed to himself rather than Lennie.

"Tried and tried," said Lennie, "but it didn't do no good. I remember about the rabbits, George."

"The hell with the rabbits. That's all you ever can remember is them rabbits. Okay! Now you listen and this time you got to remember so we don't get in no trouble. You remember sittin' in that gutter on Howard Street and watchin' that blackboard?" George recounted quickly. Lennie's face broke into a delighted smile.

"Why sure, George. I remember that … but … what do we do then? I remember some girls come by and you says … you says …" Lennie began, balling his face up and thinking hard.

"The hell with what I says. You remember about us goin' into the Doctors, Romero and Russo? Well, they signed off our quarantine cards and we got bus tickets?" George asserted, half-asking and half-explaining.

"Oh, sure, George. I remember that now," Lennie nodded. His hands went quickly into his side coat pockets. He said gently and sorrowfully, "George … I ain't got mine. I must of lost it."

He looked down at the ground in despair.

"You never had none, you crazy bastard. I got both of them here. Think I'd let you carry your own quarantine card?" George scoffed. Lennie grinned with relief.

"I ... I thought I put it in my side pocket," Lennie said, his hand still hovering over the pocket he clearly thought they were in. His hand went into the pocket again.

George looked sharply at him and questioned, "What did you take outta that pocket?"

"Ain't a thin' in my pocket," Lennie conceded cleverly.

"I know there ain't. You got it in your hand. What you got in your hand – hidin' it?" George challenged as if he had seen this trick a thousand times before.

"I ain't got nothin', George. Honest," Lennie said as innocently as he could muster.

"Come on, give it here," George demanded, not giving an inch. Lennie held his closed hand away from George's direction.

"It's only a thumb, George," Lennie explained, like it was the most normal thing in the world.

"A thumb? A human thumb?" George questioned in disbelief.

"Uh-uh. Just a dead thumb, George. I didn't break it off. Honest! I found it. I found it dead," Lennie explained, failing to see the issue at hand.

"Give it here!" demanded George with a grimace.

"Aw, let me have it, George!" Lennie pleaded.

"Give it here!" George demanded again and sticking out his hand expectantly. Lennie's closed hand slowly obeyed. George took the thumb, the cold and somewhat wet flesh cool in his hand, and threw it across the pool to the other side and among the brush.

"What you want with a dead thumb, anyways?" George asked, shaking his head and wiping his hand on his jacket.

"I could hold it in my hand while we walked along," said Lennie. "It's soft and squishy."

"Well, you ain't holdin' no dead thumb while you walk with me. You remember where we're goin' now?" George said, rolling his eyes. Lennie looked startled and then in embarrassment hid his face against his knees.

"I forgot again," he admitted solemnly.

"Jesus Christ," George said resignedly. "Well ... look, we're gonna work on a ranch like the one we come from east."

"East?" Lennie questioned.

"In Monroeville," George said bitingly.

"Oh, sure. I remember. In Monroeville," Lennie said with a lightbulb recognition moment.

"That ranch we're goin' to is right down there about a quarter mile. We're gonna go in and see the Boss. Now, look ... I'll give him the quarantine cards, but you ain't gonna say a word. You just stand there and don't say nothin'. If he finds out about the bite, we won't get no job and will prolly be killed, but if he sees you work, we're set. You got that?" George related harshly.

"Sure, George. Sure I got it," Lennie replied with an optimistic smile.

"Okay. Now when we go in to see the Boss, what you gonna do?" George said slowly and deliberately.

"I ... I ..." Lennie said laboriously. His face grew tight with thought. "I ... ain't gonna say nothin'. Just gonna stand there."

"Good boy. That's swell! You say that over two, three times so you sure won't forget it," George said, a smile of relief breaking out over his face.

Lennie droned to himself softly, "I ain't gonna say nothin' … I ain't gonna say nothin' … I ain't gonna say nothin'."

"Okay," said George, "and you ain't gonna do no bad thin's like you done in Monroeville, neither."

Lennie looked puzzled and asked, "Like I done in Monroeville?"

"Oh, so you forgot that too, did ya? Well, I ain't gonna remind ya, fear you do it again," George scoffed. A light of understanding broke on Lennie's face.

"They run us outta Monroeville," Lennie exploded triumphantly.

"Run us out, hell," said George disgustedly. "We run. They was lookin' for us, but they didn't catch us."

Lennie giggled happily. "I didn't forget that you bet."

George lay back on the sand and crossed his hands under his head, and Lennie imitated him, raising his head to see whether he was doing it right.

"God, you're a lot of trouble," said George, shaking his head. "I could get along so easy and so nice if I didn't have you on my tail. I could move quick and safe. I could live so easy and maybe have a girl. Make money off huntin' Sick Ones."

For a moment Lennie lay quiet, and then he said hopefully, "We gonna work on a ranch, George."

"Alright. You got that. But we're gonna sleep here 'cause I got a reason," George said dismissively.

The day was going fast now. Only the tops of the Gabilan Mountains flamed with the light of the sun that had gone from the valley. A water snake slipped along on the pool, its head held up like a little periscope. The reeds jerked slightly in the current. Far off toward the highway, a man shouted something and an undead man snarled back. There was a single gunshot.

"George … why ain't we goin' on to the ranch and get some supper? They got supper at the ranch," Lennie said, almost sadly. George rolled on his side and clasped his Luger.

"No reason at all for you. I like it here. Tomorrow we're gonna go to work. I seen threshin' machines on the way down. Heard a lot of shots too. That means we'll be buckin' grain bags, bustin' a gut, but prolly mostly defendin' ourselves. Tonight I'm gonna lay right here and look up. I like it," George explained calmly.

Lennie got up on his knees and looked down at George, asking, "Ain't we gonna have no supper?"

"Sure we are, if you gather up some dead willow sticks. I got three cans of beans in my bindle. You get a fire ready. I'll give you a match when you get the sticks together. Then we'll heat the beans and have supper," George said, looking at Lennie.

Lennie said, "I like beans with ketchup."

"Well, we ain't got no ketchup. You go get wood. And don't you fool around. It'll be dark before long," George snapped angrily. Lennie lumbered to his feet and disappeared in the brush. George lay where he was and whistled softly to himself, careful of the volume for fear of what it could attract. There were sounds of splashing down the river in the direction Lennie had taken. George stopped whistling and listened. He said softly, "Poor bastard."

Then went on whistling again.

In a moment Lennie came crashing back through the brush. He carried one small willow stick in his hand. George sat up.

"Alright," George said brusquely, "give me that thumb!"

But Lennie made an elaborate pantomime of innocence.

"What thumb, George? I only got my two thumbs," Lennie said innocently.

George held out his hand and demanded, "Come on. Give it to me. You ain't puttin' nothin' over."

Lennie hesitated, backed away, looked wildly at the brush line as though he contemplated running for his freedom.

George threatened coldly, "You gonna give me that thumb or do I have to sock you?"

"Give you what, George?" Lennie asked again, still trying to play dumb.

"You know goddamn well what. I want that thumb!" George almost shouted, before he remembered that undead may be nearby. Lennie reluctantly reached into his pocket.

His voice broke a little and he whispered, "I don't know why I can't keep it. It ain't nobody's thumb no more. I didn't steal it. I found it lyin' right beside the road."

George's hand remained outstretched imperiously. Slowly, like a terrier who doesn't want to bring a ball to its master, Lennie approached, drew back, approached again. George snapped his fingers sharply and, at the sound, Lennie laid the thumb in his hand. George looked around to see if the commotion had attracted unwanted attention. It hadn't.

"I wasn't doin' nothin' bad with it, George. Just holdin' it. It makes me feel safe. Like someone holdin' my hand," Lennie explained dejectedly. George stood up and threw the thumb as far as he could into the darkening brush, and then he stepped to the pool and washed his hands.

"You crazy fool. Don't you think I could see your feet was wet where you went across the river to get it?" George questioned, anger building. He heard Lennie's whimpering cry and wheeled about and glared at Lennie, "Blubberin' like a baby! Jesus Christ! A big guy like you."

Lennie's lip quivered and tears started in his eyes.

"Bu-bu—" Lennie blubbered.

"Aw, Lennie!" George put his hand on Lennie's shoulder.

"I ain't takin' it away just for meanness. That thumb ain't fresh, Lennie. Besides, it ain't even livin'. I got two thumbs, and I'll let you hold mine for a little while when we walk if you like."

Lennie sat down on the ground and hung his head dejectedly.

Lennie sadly whispered, "I liked that other thumb. It was pretty and had a pink nail. I remember a lady used to give them to me – every time there was a Sick One. But that lady ain't here."

George scoffed, "Lady, huh? Don't even remember who that lady was. That lady was tryna get you sick. And she stopped givin' them to you 'cause she got sick by touchin' them herself."

Lennie looked sadly up at him.

"They were so soft," he said, apologetically. "I'd like the soft skin and pretty soon they fell apart. I tried to pinch it back together but it won't no good. I wish we'd get the rabbits pretty soon, George. They ain't so little."

"The hell with the rabbits. And you ain't to be trusted with no live or dead nothin'. You only like the stuff when you can be too rough with it," George scoffed.

"Livin' stuff just breaks too easy," Lennie admitted sadly.

The flame of the sunset lifted from the mountaintops and dusk came into the valley, and a half-darkness came in among the willows and the sycamores. A big carp rose to the surface of the pool, gulped air and then sank mysteriously into the dark water again, leaving widening rings on the water. Overhead the leaves whisked again and little puffs of willow cotton blew down and landed on the pool's surface.

"You gonna get that wood?" George demanded after a while. "There's plenty right up against the back of that sycamore. Floodwater wood. Now you get it."

Lennie went behind the tree unquestioningly and brought out a litter of dried leaves and twigs. He threw them in a heap on the old ash pile and went back for more and more. It was almost night now. A dove's wings whistled over the water. George walked to the fire pile and lit the dry leaves with one of his few remaining matches. The flame cracked up among the twigs and fell to work. Suddenly, George was met with a terrible smell as the flames climbed. He turned to the pile and proceeded to kick one of the *sticks* out.

"Dammit Lennie!" George cursed as he removed the decaying *human* limb from the pile. He tossed it before Lennie could claim one the digits. George shook his head disgustedly, undid his bindle and brought out three cans of beans. He stood them about the fire, close in against the blaze, but not quite touching the flame.

"There's enough beans for four men," George said. Lennie watched him from over the fire.

He said patiently, "I like them with ketchup."

"Well, we ain't got any," George exploded. "Whatever we ain't got, that's what you want! God almighty, if I was alone I could live so easy. I could go get a job and work, and no trouble. No mess at all, and when the end of the month come I could take my fifty bucks and go into town and get whatever I want. Why, I could stay in a cat house all night. I could eat any place I want, hotel or any place, and order any damn thing I could think of. Could pay for somewhere safer if it was just me. And I could do all that every damn month. Get a gallon of whisky, or sit in a pool room and play cards or shoot pool."

Lennie knelt and looked over the fire at the angry George, and Lennie's face was drawn with terror.

"But I—" Lennie began, but George wasn't done.

"And what have I got? I got you! You can't keep a job and you lose me every job I get. Just keep me shovin' all over the country all the time. And that ain't the worst. You get in trouble. You get bit and I got to get you out," George went on furiously. His voice rose nearly to a shout. "You crazy son-of-a-bitch. You keep me in hot water all the time."

Lennie tried to speak but George carried on breathlessly. He took on the elaborate manner of little girls when they are mimicking one another, "Just wanted to hold the sick girl's hand – just wanted to hold her thumb. Well, what did you think would happen? People were keepin' away from her for a reason! She bites and we got to hide in an irrigation ditch all day with guys lookin' for us, and we got to sneak out in the dark and get outta the country. All the time somethin' like that. All the time. I wish I could put you in a cage with about a million thumbs and let you have fun."

His anger left him suddenly. He looked across the fire at Lennie's anguished face, and then he looked ashamedly at the flames.

It was quite dark now, but the fire lit the trunks of the trees and the curving branches overhead. Lennie crawled slowly and cautiously around the fire until he was close to George. He sat back on his heels. George turned the bean cans so that another side faced the fire. He pretended to be unaware of Lennie so close beside him.

"George," Lennie said very softly. No answer. He spoke again but louder, "George!"

"What do you want?" George sighed.

"I was only foolin', George. I don't want no ketchup. I wouldn't eat no ketchup if it was right here beside me," Lennie said apologetically.

"If it was here, you could have some," George said, feeling guilty.

"But I wouldn't eat none, George. I'd leave it all for you. You could cover your beans with it and I wouldn't touch none of it," Lennie said with a smile.

George still stared morosely at the fire and said with a sigh, "When I think of the swell time I could have without you, I go nuts. I never get no peace."

Lennie still knelt. He looked off into the darkness across the river.

"George, you want I should go away and leave you alone?" Lennie questioned. "I could hide away."

"Where the hell could you go?" George said with scorn.

"Well, I could. I could go off in the hills there. Someplace I'd find a cave," Lennie said, casting his mind to his imaginary future.

"Yeah? How'd you eat? You ain't got sense enough to find nothin' to eat. Soon enough you'd be eatin' man-flesh anyways," George said, squinting at Lennie.

"I'd find thin's, George. I don't need no nice food with ketchup. I'd lay out in the sun and nobody would hurt me. And if I found a thumb, I could keep it. Nobody would take it away from me," Lennie said excitedly. Then added, almost as an afterthought, "What you mean man-flesh?"

"You really don't get it, do you?" George said shaking his head, then looked quickly and searchingly at him. "I been mean, ain't I?"

"If you don't want me I can go off in the hills and find a cave. I can go away any time," Lennie repeated.

"No … look! I was just foolin', Lennie. 'Cause I want you to stay with me. Trouble with thumbs is they come from people," He paused. "Tell you what I'll do, Lennie. First chance I get I'll give you a pup. It ain't no thumb and don't got no thumbs, but you can touch it. Maybe you wouldn't kill it. That would be better than a thumb. And it won't make you sick."

Lennie avoided the bait. He had sensed his advantage.

He said with a sly smile, "If you don't want me, you only just got to say so, and I'll go off in those hills right there. Right up in those hills and live by myself. And I won't get no thumbs stole from me."

George said, "I want you to stay with me, Lennie. Jesus Christ, somebody would shoot you for a Sick One if you was by yourself. No, you stay with me. I can't have you runnin' off by yourself; you'd get dead."

Lennie spoke craftily, "Tell me … like you done before."

"Tell you what?" George said, narrowing his eyes at Lennie.

"About the rabbits," Lennie said, barely able to contain his joy.

George snapped, "You ain't gonna put nothin' over on me."

Lennie pleaded, "Come on, George. Tell me. Please, George. Like you done before."

"You get a kick outta that, don't you? Alright, I'll tell you, and then we'll eat our supper …" George said, sitting up. George's voice became deeper. He repeated his words rhythmically as though he had said them many times before. "Guys like us that work on ranches are the most at risk guys in the world. They got no family to help them. No friends either. They don't belong no place. They come to a ranch and work up a stake, killin' the Sick Ones and then they go into town and blow their stake, and the first thing you know they're poundin' their tail on some other ranch. If they don't get ate first. They ain't got nothin' to look ahead to."

Lennie was delighted, and interrupted excitely, "That's it! That's it! Now tell how it is with us."

George went on. "With us, it ain't like that. We got a future. We got somebody to talk to that gives a damn about us. We don't have to sit in no bar room blowin' in our jack just 'cause we got no place else to go. If them other guys gets turned, they can rot and get shot for all anybody gives a damn. But not us."

Lennie broke in animatedly, "But not us! And why? 'Cause … 'cause I got you to look after me, and you got me to look after you, and that's why. Go on now, George!"

He laughed delightedly.

"You got it by heart. You can do it yourself," George said with a tight-lipped smile.

"No, you. I forget some of the things. Tell about how it's gonna be," Lennie begged.

George smiled, more genuinely this time and continued, "Okay. Someday, we're gonna get the jack together and we're gonna have a little house and a couple of acres and a big wall and—"

"And live offa fatta the lan'!" Lennie shouted. "And have rabbits. Go on, George! Tell about what we're gonna have in the garden and about the rabbits in the cages and about the Sick Ones and the stove, and how thick the cream is on the milk like you can hardly cut it. Tell about that, George."

"Why don't you do it yourself? You know all of it," George said with a nod towards Lennie.

"No ... you tell it. It ain't the same if I tell it. Go on ... George. How I get to tend the rabbits," Lennie begged again.

"Well. We'll have a big vegetable patch and a rabbit hutch and chickens. And if there's too many Sick Ones outside that day, we'll just say the hell with goin' to work, and we'll build up a fire in the stove and sit around it and listen to the moans comin' from outside the wall ... Nuts!" said George before ending sharply on the final word. He took out his pocket knife and added sourly, "I ain't got time for no more."

He drove his knife through the top of one of the bean cans, sawed out the top and passed the can to Lennie. Then he opened a second can. From his side pocket, he brought out two spoons and passed one of them to Lennie.

They sat by the fire and filled their mouths with beans and chewed mightily. A few beans slipped out of the side of Lennie's mouth. George wondered if it was the spasmodic movement that first came with the infection when it rooted in the blood.

George gestured with his spoon and asked, "What you gonna say tomorrow when the Boss asks you questions?"

Lennie stopped chewing and swallowed. His face was concentrated and said with difficulty, "I ... I ain't gonna ... say a word."

"Good boy! That's fine, Lennie! Maybe you're gettin' better. When we get the couple of acres I can let you tend the rabbits all right. Especially if you remember as good as that," George grinned happily.

Lennie choked with pride and said, "I can remember."

George motioned with his spoon again and said with an edge of desperation, "Look, Lennie. I want you to look around here. You can remember this place, can't you? The ranch is about a quarter mile up that way. Just follow the river?"

"Sure," said Lennie. "I can remember this. Didn't I remember about not gonna say a word?"

"Course you did. Well, look. Lennie … if you just happen to get in trouble like you always done before, I want you to come right here and hide in the brush," George repeated forcefully, trying to reiterate the point.

"Hide in the brush," said Lennie slowly.

"Hide in the brush till I come for you. Don't let no Sick Ones see ya, nor any people. Can you remember that?" George commanded.

"Sure I can, George. Hide in the brush till you come. No people. No Sick Ones," Lennie said with a nod.

"But you ain't gonna get in no trouble, 'cause if you do, I won't let you tend the rabbits," George said, finalising his instructions with a threat. He threw his empty bean can off into the brush.

"I won't get in no trouble, George. I ain't gonna say a word," Lennie said pridefully.

"Okay. Brin' your bindle over here by the fire. It's gonna be nice sleepin' here, lookin' up, and the leaves. Don't build up no more fire or we'll get seen. We'll let her die down," George instructed.

They made their beds on the sand, and as the blaze dropped from the fire the sphere of light grew smaller; the curling branches disappeared and only a faint glimmer showed where the tree trunks were.

From the darkness, Lennie called, "George, you asleep?"

"No. What do you want?" George replied, clearly having been asleep.

"Let's have different colour rabbits, George," Lennie said, and George knew he was smiling even in the dark.

"Sure we will," George said sleepily. "Red and blue and green rabbits, Lennie. Millions of them."

"Furry ones, George, like I seen in the fair in Sacramento," Lennie said, as if he was reminding George.

"Sure, furry ones," George replied, riding the twilight of sleep.

"Cause I can just as well go away, George, and live in a cave," Lennie said, almost as a threat, blackmailing George into having red, blue and green furry rabbits.

"You can just as well go to hell," George snapped. "Shut up now."

The red light dimmed on the coals. Up the hill from the river, there was another gunshot and a gun of a different calibre answered from the other side of the stream. The sycamore leaves whispered in a little night breeze.

CHAPTER 2

The bunkhouse was a long, rectangular building. Inside, the walls were whitewashed and the floor unpainted. Just because the floor was unpainted, did not mean it was unclean; there were patches of dark brown on it, caused by spilt blood that had been scrubbed repeatedly to remove whatever they could. In three walls there were small, square windows, and in the fourth, a solid door with a wooden latch. A metal bar across the door and wire mesh crisscrossing the windows appeared to be recent additions. Against the walls were eight bunks, five of them made up with blankets and the other three showing their burlap ticking. Until recently the three beds had been occupied, but that had changed due to an incident related to the spilt blood and the new security measures. Over each bunk, there was nailed an apple box with the opening forward so that it made two shelves for the personal belongings of the occupant of the bunk. These shelves were loaded with little articles, soap, Luger rounds, razors and those Western magazines ranch men love to read and scoff at yet secretly believe. There were medicines on the shelves – little vials and combs. From nails on the box sides, a few neckties. Near one wall there was a black cast-iron stove, its stovepipe going straight up through the ceiling. In the middle of the room stood a big square table littered with playing cards, and around it were grouped boxes for the players to sit on.

The journey from George and Lennie's campsite to the bunkhouse was without fatal incident – there was a momentary exchange of gunfire between George and another individual who mistook Lennie's lumbering form following George as a chase between the undead and the living. It was only when the would-be saviour was returned fire upon that he realised his mistake. Cans of beans were given by way of an apology and both groups continued on their way without a further exchange of words or bullets. Lennie and George reached the ranch, which looked like so many they had worked on, and went to the bunkhouse.

At about ten o'clock in the morning the sun threw a bright dust-laden bar through one of the side windows, and in and out of the beam flies shot like rushing stars. The wooden latch raised and the bar slid across. The door opened and a tall, stoop-shouldered old man came in. He was dressed in blue jeans and he carried a big push-broom in his left hand. Behind him came George, and behind George, Lennie.

"The Boss was expectin' you last night. He was sore as hell when you wasn't here to go out this mornin'," the old man said. He pointed with his right arm, and out of the sleeve came a round stick-like wrist, but no hand. He indicated two beds near the stove and said. "You can have them two beds there."

George stepped over and threw his blankets down on the burlap sack of straw that was a mattress. They were the furthest away from the other residents and George wondered if that was the normal thing for all new workers. He looked into his box shelf and then picked a small yellow can from it.

"Say. What the hell's this?" George said, anger beginning to form.

"I don't know," said the old man, squinting at the can.

"Says 'Positively kills lice, roaches and any carriers of infection.' What the hell kind of bed you givin' us, anyways? We don't want no pants rabbits," George spat angrily. The old Swamper shifted his broom and held it between his elbow and his side while he held out his hand for the can. He studied the label carefully.

"Tell you what," he said finally after contemplating the can, "the last guy that had this bed was a blacksmith, hell of a nice fella and as clean a guy as you wanta meet. Used to wash his hands even after he ate."

"Then how come he worried about infection?" George said, working up a slow anger on top of the spark that had already formed. Lennie put his bindle on the neighbouring bunk and sat down. He watched George with an open mouth.

"Tell you what," said the old Swamper. "This here blacksmith, name of Whitey, was the kind of guy that would put that stuff around even if there wasn't no bugs. Just to make sure, see? Tell you what he used to do … at meals, he'd peel his boiled potatoes, and he'd take out every little spot, no matter what kind, before he ate it. And if there was a red splotch on an egg, he'd scrape it off. Finally, he quit. That's the kinda guy he was – clean. Used to go up Sundays even when he wasn't goin' no place, put on a necktie even, and then sit in the bunkhouse."

"I ain't so sure," said George sceptically. "What did you say he quit for?"

The old man put the yellow can in his pocket, and he rubbed his bristly white whiskers with his knuckles and said, "Why … he … just quit life. The way a guy will nowadays. Says it was the world. Just wanted to quit. Didn't give no other reason but the world. Just says 'Gimme my time' one night, the way any guy would. Blew his brains out the other week in the barn."

George lifted his tick and looked underneath it. He leaned over and inspected the sacking closely. Immediately Lennie got up and did the same with his bed. Finally, George seemed satisfied. He unrolled his bindle and put things on the shelf, his razor and bar of soap, his Luger, a bottle of pills for Lennie's fever, his liniment and leather wristband. Then he made his bed up neatly with blankets.

The old man said, "I guess the Boss will be out here in a minute. He was sure burned when you wasn't here this mornin'. Come right in when we was eatin' breakfast and says, 'Where the hell's them new men?' And he give the stable buck hell, too."

George patted a wrinkle out of his bed and sat down.

"Give the stable buck hell?" George asked.

"Sure. You see the stable buck's a nigger," the Swamper said by way of an explanation.

"Nigger, huh?" George said, nodding.

"Yeah. Nice fella too. Got a crooked back where a Sick One tried to drag him away. The Boss gives him hell when he's mad. But the stable buck don't give a damn about that. He reads a lot. Got books in his room," the Swamper said, a flood of words exploding from his mouth now that he had someone to listen.

"What kind of a guy is the Boss?" George asked.

"Well, he's a pretty nice fella. Gets pretty mad sometimes, but he's pretty nice. Tell you what, know what he done when the Walkin' Plague started? Brang a gallon of whisky right in here and says, 'Drink hearty, boys. The world only ends once'," the Swamper explained.

"The hell he did! Whole gallon?" George asked in disbelief.

"Yes, sir. Jesus, we had fun. They let the nigger come in that night. Little skinner name of Smitty took after the nigger. Done pretty good, too. The guys wouldn't let him use his feet, so the nigger got him. If he coulda used his feet, Smitty says he woulda killed the nigger. The guys said on account of the nigger's got a crooked back, Smitty can't use his feet," the Swamper said. He paused in relish of the memory. He added with a smile, "After that, the guys went into Soledad and raised hell. I didn't go in there. I ain't got the poop no more. Can't defend myself with just one hand."

Lennie was just finishing making his bed. The wooden latch raised again and the door opened. A little stocky man stood in the open doorway. He wore blue jean trousers, a flannel shirt, a black, unbuttoned vest and a black coat. His thumbs were stuck in his belt, on each side of a square steel buckle; a revolver rested on each hip. On his head was a soiled brown Stetson hat, and he wore high-heeled boots and spurs to prove he was not a labouring man. The old Swamper looked quickly at him, stiffened and then shuffled to the door rubbing his whiskers with his knuckles as he went.

"Them guys just come," he said and shuffled past the Boss and out the door. The Boss stepped into the room with the short, quick steps of a fat-legged man.

"I wrote Romero and Russo I wanted two men this mornin'. Two *well* men. You got your quarantine cards?" the Boss demanded, temper short. George reached into his pocket and produced the cards and handed them to the Boss who studied them intensely. His eyes narrowed and he said to George, "It wasn't Romero and Russo's fault. Says right here on the card that you was fit to be here for work this mornin'.

Makes your card outdated. Anythin' coulda happened between there and here. Coulda got bit. Quarantine don't mean anythin' if it's outdated."

George looked down at his feet and said, "Bus driver give us a bum steer. We had to walk ten miles. Says we was here when we wasn't. We couldn't get no rides in the mornin'."

The Boss squinted his eyes again.

"Well, I had to send out the grain teams short two shooters. No one to protect them. Won't do any good to go out now till after dinner, they're too far to catch up and they'll be finishin' up soon," the Boss said with annoyance. He pulled his time-book out of his pocket and opened it where a pencil was stuck between the leaves. George scowled meaningfully at Lennie, and Lennie nodded to show that he understood. The Boss licked his pencil and said carefully, "What's your name?"

"George Milton," George replied curtly.

"And what's yours?" the Boss said turning to Lennie.

George quickly said, "His name's Lennie Small."

The names were entered in the book.

"Let's see, this is the twentieth, noon the twentieth," the Boss said thoughtfully. He closed the book. "Where you boys been workin'?"

"Up around Monroeville," said George.

"You, too?" he asked Lennie.

"Yeah, him too," said George.

The Boss pointed a playful finger at Lennie and said with a knowing smile, "He ain't much of a talker, is he?"

"No, he ain't, but he's sure as hell good at tossin' the Sick Ones. Strong as a bull. Seen him pull a head clean off," George said enthusiastically. Lennie smiled to himself.

"Strong as a bull," he repeated. George scowled at him, and Lennie dropped his head in shame at having forgotten.

"Listen, Small!" the Boss said suddenly, Lennie raised his head. "What can you do?"

In a panic, Lennie looked at George for help.

"He can do anythin' you tell him," said George, panic beginning to enter his mind. "He's good with an axe. Prefers to use his hands though. He can carry the bodies, move them far away. He can do anythin'. Just give him a try."

The Boss turned on George and snapped, "Then why don't you let him answer? What you tryna put over?"

George broke in loudly, "Oh! I ain't sayin' he's bright. He ain't. But I say he's a goddamn good worker. He can put up a couple of hundred pound bodies over his shoulders. Ain't no problem."

The Boss deliberately put the little book in his pocket. He hooked his thumbs in his belt and squinted one eye nearly closed.

The Boss questioned suspiciously, "Say what you sellin'?"

"Huh?" George responded with surprise.

"I said what stake you got in this guy? You takin' his pay away from him?" The Boss pushed, sensing something amiss.

"No, course I ain't. Why you think I'm sellin' him out?" George replied with disgust.

"Well, I never seen one guy take so much trouble for another guy. I just like to know what your interest is," the Boss explained, sensing he had almost pushed a good man too far but still reluctant to let up.

George said, "He's my … cousin. I told his old lady I'd take care of him. He got kicked in the head by a horse when he was a kid. He's alright. Just ain't bright. But he can do anythin' you tell him."

The Boss turned partly away and said, "Well, God knows he don't need any brains to crack skulls, but don't you try to put nothin' over, Milton. I got my eye on you. Why did you quit in Monroeville?"

"Job was done," said George promptly.

"What kinda job?" the Boss fired back.

"We … we was chasin' dead ones outta town," George replied, momentarily hesitating.

"All right. But don't try to put nothin' over, 'cause you can't get away with nothin'. I seen wise guys before. Go on out with the grain teams after dinner. They're pickin' up barley at the threshin' machine. Go out with Slim's team. Protect them," the Boss demanded calmly.

"Slim?" George questioned.

"Yeah. Big tall skinner. You'll see him at dinner," the Boss replied. He turned abruptly and went to the door but, before he went out, he turned and looked for a long moment at the two men. "You ain't bit are ya?"

Before George could answer, or Lennie could react, he laughed and left.

When the sound of his footsteps had died away, George turned on Lennie and said, "So you wasn't gonna say a word? You was gonna leave your big flapper shut and leave me to do the talkin'? Damn near lost us the job."

Lennie stared hopelessly at his hands and said desperately, "I forgot, George."

"Yeah, you forgot. You always forget, and I got to talk you out of it. Now he's got his eye on us. Now we got to be careful and not make no slips. You keep your big flapper shut after this," George ranted and sat down heavily on the bunk. He fell morosely silent before adding quietly, "and keep your arm covered. He don't need to see no bite."

"George?" Lennie said with a quizzical tone.

"What you want now?" George sighed, pinching the bridge of his nose.

"I wasn't kicked in the head with no horse, was I, George?" Lennie asked, as if trying to remember the event and failing.

"Be a damn good thin' if you was," George said viciously. "Save everybody a hell of a lot of trouble."

"You said I was your cousin, George," Lennie said with an excited smile.

"Well, that was a lie. And I'm damn glad it was. If I was a relative of yours I'd shoot myself," George said with exasperation. He stopped suddenly, stepped to the open front door and peered out. He suddenly said, voice full of malice, "Say, what the hell you doin' listenin'?"

The old man came slowly into the room. He had his broom in his hand. At his heels there walked a dragfooted sheepdog, grey of muzzle, and with pale, blind old eyes. The dog struggled lamely to the side of the room and lay down, grunting softly to himself and licking his grizzled, moth-eaten coat. The Swamper watched him until he was settled.

"I wasn't listenin'. I was just standin' in the shade a minute scratchin' my dog. I just now finished swampin' out the wash house," the Swamper tried to explain.

"You was pokin' your big ears into our business," George said angrily. "I don't like nobody to get nosey."

The old man looked uneasily from George to Lennie, and then back.

"I just come there," he said with a heavy shrug. "I didn't hear nothin' you guys was sayin'. I ain't interested in nothin' you was sayin'. A guy on a ranch don't never listen nor he don't ask no questions."

"Damn right he don't, not if he wants to stay workin' long," said George, slightly mollified and reassured by the Swamper's defence. He then said, a lot calmer, "Come on in and sit down a minute. That's a hell of an old dog."

"Yeah. I had him ever since he was a pup. God, he was a good sheepdog when he was younger," he said nostalgically. He stood his broom against the wall and he rubbed his white bristled cheek with his knuckles. He asked, "How'd you like the Boss?"

"Pretty good. Seemed alright," George replied with a nod.

"He's a nice fella," the Swamper agreed. "You got to take him right."

At that moment a young man came into the bunkhouse; a thin young man with a brown face, with brown eyes and a head of tightly curled hair. He wore a work glove on his left hand and, like the Boss, he wore high-heeled boots.

"Seen my old man?" he asked.

The Swamper said, "He was here just a minute ago, Curley. Went over to the cookhouse, I think."

"I'll try to catch him," said Curley. His eyes passed over the new men and he stopped. He glanced coldly at George and then at Lennie. His arms gradually bent at the elbows and his hands closed into fists. He stiffened and went into a slight crouch. His glance was at once calculating and pugnacious. Lennie squirmed under the look and shifted his feet nervously. Curley stepped gingerly close to him.

"You the new guys the old man was waitin' for?" Curley snarled.

"We just come in," said George.

"Let the big guy talk," Curley snapped in reply. Lennie twisted with embarrassment.

George said, "S'pose he don't wanta talk?"

Curley lashed his body around and growled, "By Christ, he's gotta talk when he's spoke to. What the hell are you gettin' into it for?"

"We travel together," said George coldly.

"Oh, so it's that way," Curley said with a cold stare. George was tense, and motionless.

"Yeah, it's *that* way," George replied slowly and deliberately. Lennie was looking helplessly to George for instruction.

"And you won't let the big guy talk, is that it?" Curley said, moving like a stalking predator.

"He can talk if he wants to tell you anythin'," George said calmly. He nodded slightly to Lennie.

"We just come in," said Lennie softly.

Curley stared levelly at him and said, "Well, next time you answer when you're spoke to."

He turned toward the door and walked out, and his elbows were still bent out a little. George watched him out, and then he turned back to the Swamper.

"Say, what the hell's he got on his shoulder? Lennie didn't do nothing to him. Actin' like Lennie is a damn Sick One," George sighed. The old man looked cautiously at the door to make sure no one was listening.

"That's the Boss's son," he said quietly. "Curley's pretty handy. He done in quite a few of the Sick Ones by himself. He's a crack shot, and he's handy."

"Well, let him be handy," spat George. "He don't have to take after Lennie. Lennie didn't do nothin' to him. What's he got against Lennie?"

The Swamper considered this comment before saying, "Well … tell you what. Curley's like a lot of little guys. He hates big guys. He's all the time pickin' scraps with big guys.

Kind of like he's mad at them 'cause he ain't a big guy. You seen little guys like that, ain't you? Always scrappy?"

"Sure," said George. "I seen plenty tough little guys. But this Curley better not make no mistakes about Lennie. Lennie ain't handy, but this Curley punk is gonna get hurt if he messes around with Lennie."

"Well, Curley's pretty handy," the Swamper said sceptically.

"Never did seem right to me. S'pose Curley jumps a big guy and licks him. Everybody says what a game guy Curley is. And s'pose he does the same thin' and gets licked. Then everybody says the big guy oughta pick somebody his own size, and maybe they gang up on the big guy. Never did seem right to me. Seems like Curley ain't givin' nobody a chance," George snapped watching the door. He added ominously, "Well, he better watch out for Lennie. Lennie ain't no crack shot, but Lennie's strong and quick and Lennie don't know no rules."

He walked to the square table and sat down on one of the boxes. He gathered some of the cards together and shuffled them. The old man sat down on another box.

"Don't tell Curley I said none of this. He'd slough me. He just don't give a damn. Won't ever get canned 'cause his old man's the Boss. More importantly, he stops the Sick Ones," the old Swamper whispered conspiratorially. George cut the cards and began turning them over, looking at each one and throwing it down on a pile.

George said, "This guy Curley sounds like a son-of-a-bitch to me. I don't like mean little guys, no matter how many Sick Ones they puts down."

"Seems to me like he's worse lately," said the Swamper. "He got married a couple of weeks ago. Wife lives over in the

Boss's house. Seems like Curley is cockier than ever since he got married."

George grunted, "Maybe he's showin' off for his wife."

The Swamper warmed to his gossip and goaded George by asking, "You seen that glove on his left hand?"

"Yeah. I seen it," George said, taking the bait nonchalantly.

"Well, that glove's fulla Vaseline," the Swamper said, barely able to contain his smile.

"Vaseline? What the hell for?" George questioned sceptically.

"Well, I tell you what – Curley says he's keepin' that hand soft for his wife. One hand for stringin' out the sick, the other for her," the Swamper explained. George studied the cards absorbedly.

"That's a dirty thin' to tell around," he said. The old man was reassured as he had drawn a derogatory statement from George. He felt safe now, and he spoke more confidently.

"Wait until you see Curley's wife," the old Swamper said, making no effort to hide his grin. George cut the cards again and put out a solitaire lay, slowly and deliberately.

"Purty?" he asked casually.

"Yeah. Purty … but—" the Swamper said, ending his statement mid-sentence.

George studied his cards. "But what?"

"Well – she got the eye," the Swamper said, nodding at George as if to communicate the unspoken meaning behind his words.

"Yeah? Married two weeks and got the eye? Maybe that's why Curley's pants is fulla ants," George said matter-of-factly.

"I seen her give Slim the eye. Slim's a jerkline skinner. Hell of a nice fella. Slim don't need to wear no high-heeled boots on a grain team. Can put a Sick One down from about quart' mile away. I seen her give Slim the eye. Curley never seen it. And I seen her give Carlson the eye," the Swamper said excitedly.

George pretended a lack of interest and, as if an afterthought, said, "Looks like we was gonna have fun."

"Know what I think?" the Swamper said as he stood up from his box. George did not answer. Then said, spitting the last two words, "Well, I think Curley's married … a tart."

"He ain't the first," said George, not looking up. "There's plenty done that."

The old man moved toward the door, and his ancient dog lifted his head and peered about, and then got painfully to his feet to follow.

"I gotta be settin' out the wash basins for the guys. The teams will be in before long," The Swamper said, and then asked George, "You guys gonna shoot Sick Ones?"

"Yeah," George said absentmindedly.

"You won't tell Curley nothin' I said?" the old man asked cautiously.

"Hell no," George exclaimed, snapping back to the present.

"Well, you look her over, mister. You see if she ain't a tart," He advised to justify his own comments. He unlocked the door and stepped out the door into the brilliant sunshine.

George laid down his cards thoughtfully, turned his piles of three. He built four clubs on his ace pile – the top one heavily bloodstained. The sun square was on the floor now, and the flies whipped through it like sparks. A sound of jingling harness and the croak of heavy-laden axles sounded from outside.

"Stable buck – ooh, sta-able buck!" George heard from the distance, and then, "Where the hell is that goddamn nigger?"

George stared at his solitaire lay, and then he flounced the cards together and turned around to Lennie. Lennie was lying down on the bunk watching him.

"Look, Lennie! This here ain't no setup. I'm scared. You gonna have trouble with that Curley guy. I seen that kind before. He was kinda feelin' you out. He figures he's got you scared and he's gonna take a sock at you the first chance he gets. Reckon he senses the bite," George warned. Lennie's eyes were frightened.

"I don't want no trouble," he said plaintively. "Don't let him sock me, George."

George got up and went over to Lennie's bunk and sat down on it.

"I hate that kinda bastard. I seen plenty of them. Like the old guy says, Curley don't take no chances. He always wins," George said, before stopping to think for a moment. "If he tangles with you, Lennie, we're gonna get the can … or worse. Don't make no mistake about that. He loves huntin' the Sick Ones. You can just tell, and that ain't normal. Look, Lennie. You try to keep away from him, will you? Don't never speak to him. If he comes in here you move clear to the other side of the room. Make sure you never show him your bite either. Will you do that, Lennie?"

"I don't want no trouble," Lennie mourned. "I never done nothin' to him."

"Well, that won't do you no good if Curley wants to plug himself up for a hunter. If he has even a whiff of a reason, nothin' will stop him. Just don't have nothin' to do with him."

Will you remember?" George explained hurriedly, trying to make Lennie understand.

"Sure, George. I ain't gonna say a word," Lennie said, nodding his head in huge dips and rises.

The sound of the approaching grain teams was louder, the thud of big hooves on the hard ground, and the drag of brakes with the jingle of trace chains. Men were calling back and forth from the teams. George, sitting on the bunk beside Lennie, frowned as he thought.

Lennie asked timidly, "You ain't mad, George?"

"I ain't mad at you. I'm mad at this here Curley bastard. I hoped we was gonna get a little stake together – maybe a hundred dollars. Maybe enough for medicine and some land," George said sadly. His tone grew decisive. "You keep away from Curley, Lennie."

"Sure I will, George. I won't say a word," Lennie said, still nodding his head.

"Don't let him pull you in … but, if the son-of-a-bitch socks you let him have it," George advised.

"Let him have what, George?" Lennie asked innocently.

"Never mind, never mind. I'll tell you when. I hate that kind of a guy. Just no bitin' or scratchin'. Look, Lennie, if you get in any kind of trouble, you remember what I told you to do?" George asked Lennie, his heart momentarily in his throat. Lennie raised up on his elbow. His face contorted with thought. Then his eyes moved sadly to George's face.

"If I get in any trouble, you ain't gonna let me tend the rabbits," Lennie recited with sorrow.

"That's not what I meant. You remember where we slept last night? Down by the river?" George said doing his best to hide his frustration and, to some degree, desperation.

"Yeah. I remember. Oh, sure I remember! I go there and hide in the brush," Lennie replied excitedly. His chest swelled with pride – his rabbits momentarily forgotten.

"Hide till I come for you. Don't let nobody see you. Hide in the brush by the river. Say that over," George said forcefully.

"Hide in the brush by the river, down in the brush by the river," Lennie said, yet still nodding.

"If you get in trouble," George reinforced.

"If I get in trouble," Lennie repeatedly. George wasn't sure if he was just echoing the words or fully comprehended what was meant.

A brake screeched outside and a call came, "Stable – buck. Oh! Sta-able buck."

George said, "Say it over to yourself, Lennie, so you won't forget it."

Both men glanced up, for the rectangle of sunshine in the doorway was cut off. A girl was standing there, silhouetted by the glow, looking in. She had full, rouged lips and wide-spaced eyes, heavily made up. Her fingernails were red. Her hair hung in little rolled clusters, like fingers. She wore a cotton house dress and red mules, on the insteps of which were little bouquets of red ostrich feathers.

"I'm lookin' for Curley," she said. Her voice had a nasal, brittle quality.

George looked away from her and then back before saying sternly, "He was in here a minute ago, but he went."

"Oh!" she put her hands behind her back and leaned against the door frame so that her body was thrown forward. "You're the new fellas that just come, ain't ya?"

"Yeah," George replied, giving nothing more than he had too. Lennie's eyes moved down over her body, and though she did not seem to be looking at Lennie she bridled a little. She looked at her fingernails.

"Sometimes Curley's in here," she explained softly.

George said brusquely, "Well he ain't now."

"If he ain't, I guess I better look someplace else," she said playfully. Lennie watched her, fascinated.

George said defensively, "If I see him, I'll pass the word you was lookin' for him."

She smiled archly and twitched her body.

"Nobody can't blame a person for lookin'," she said. There were footsteps behind her going by. She turned her head and said, "Hi, Slim."

Slim's voice came through the door, "Hi, Good-lookin'."

"I'm tryna find Curley, Slim," she replied.

"Well, you ain't tryin' very hard. I seen him goin' in your house," Slim replied simply. She was suddenly apprehensive.

"Bye, boys," she called into the bunkhouse, and she hurried away. George looked around at Lennie.

"Jesus, what a tramp," George said. "So that's what Curley picks for a wife."

"She's purty," said Lennie defensively.

"Yeah, and she's sure hidin' it. Curley got his work ahead of him. Bet she'd clear out for twenty bucks. I'd rather fight Sick Ones then deal with the trouble that will follow her," George said shaking his head.

Lennie still stared at the doorway where she had been.

"Gosh, she was purty," He said again and smiled admiringly. George looked quickly down at him and then he took him by an ear and shook him.

"Listen to me, you crazy bastard," he said fiercely. "Don't you even take a look at that bitch! I don't care what she says and what she does. I seen them poison before, but I never seen no piece of jailbait worse than her. You leave her be."

Lennie tried to disengage his ear.

"I never done nothin', George," Lennie wept, big fat tears rolling down his cheeks.

"No, you never. But when she was standin' in the doorway showin' her legs, you wasn't lookin' the other way, neither," George hissed.

"I never meant no harm, George. Honest I never," Lennie pleaded.

"Well, you keep away from her, 'cause she's a rat trap if I ever seen one. You let Curley take the rap. He let himself in for it. 'Crack shot'," George said disgustedly. "And I bet he's keepin' Sick Ones scalps like some sorta trophy. Bet he ain't ever killed one up close."

Lennie cried out suddenly, "I don't like this place, George. This ain't no good place. I wanna get outta here."

"We gotta keep it till we get a stake. We can't help it, Lennie. We'll get out just as soon as we can. I don't like it no better than you do. Bet it's a lot safer here than out there," George explained, gesturing to the wider world with his hand. He went back to the table and set out a new solitaire hand. He added, "No, I don't like it. For two bits I'd shove out of here. If we can get just a few dollars in the poke we'll shove off and go up the American River and hunt Sick Ones. We can make maybe a couple of dollars a day doin' that if we turn in proof."

Lennie leaned eagerly toward him and whispered, "Let's go, George. Let's get outta here. It's mean here."

"We gotta stay," George said shortly. "Shut up now. The guys will be comin' in."

From the washroom nearby came the sound of running water and rattling basins. George studied the cards.

44

"Maybe we oughta wash up," George said after a while. "But we ain't done nothin' to get dirty. Then again … don't wanna get sick."

Then, a tall man appeared in the doorway. He held a crushed Stetson hat under his arm while he combed his long, black, damp hair straight back. Like the others, he wore blue jeans and a short denim jacket. There were brown splotches across his clothes – dried and washed out blood. When he had finished combing his hair he moved into the room, and he moved with a majesty achieved only by royalty and master craftsmen. He was a jerkline skinner, the prince of the ranch and knight of the realm, capable of felling ten, sixteen, even twenty undead and never breaking line. He was capable of shooting one of the undead as it chased the living with never a fear of missing his target. There was an earned gravity in his manner and a quiet so profound that all talk stopped when he spoke. His authority was so great that his word was taken on any subject, be it life or death. This was Slim, the people's hero. His hatchet face was ageless. He might have been thirty-five or fifty, yet his eyes carried the weight of a thousand long winters. His ear heard more than was said to him and his slow speech had overtones, not of thought but, of understanding beyond his years. He had contemplated death and the undead, and accepted the truth he had arrived at with the gravitas of Friedrich Wilhelm Nietzsche considering the battle with monsters. His hands, large and lean, were as delicate in their action as those of a temple dancer. He smoothed out his crushed hat, creased it in the middle and put it on. He looked kindly at the two in the bunkhouse.

"It's brighter than a bitch outside," he said gently. "Can't hardly see nothin' in here. You the new guys?"

"Just come," said George.

"Gonna shoot Sick Ones?" Slim asked calmly.

"That's what the Boss says," George nodded. Slim sat down on a box across the table from George. He studied the solitaire hand that was upside down to him.

"Hope you get on my team," he said. His voice was very gentle. "I gotta pair of punks on my team that don't know their own asshole from a Luger barrel. You guys ever kill a Sick One?"

"Hell, yes," said George. "I ain't nothin' to scream about, but that big bastard there can tear the head off a Sick One like a cork out a bottle."

Lennie, who had been following the conversation back and forth with his eyes, smiled complacently at the compliment. Slim looked approvingly at George for having given the compliment. He leaned over the table and snapped the corner of a loose card.

"You guys travel around together?" Slim asked, his tone was friendly and it invited confidence without demanding it. There was something about his words that made George warm to him, like there was no hidden agenda or ulterior motive to what he spoke; everything he said was exactly what he meant.

"Sure. We kinda look after each other," George said and indicated Lennie with his thumb. "He ain't bright. Hell of a good worker, though. Hell of a nice fella, but he ain't bright. I've knew him for a long time."

Slim looked through George and beyond him.

He mused, "Ain't many guys travel around together. I don't know why. Maybe everybody in the whole damn world is scared of each other."

"It's a lot safer to go around with a guy you know," said George. A powerful, big-stomached man came into the bunkhouse. His head still dripped water from the scrubbing and dousing.

"Hi, Slim," he said, and then stopped and stared at George and Lennie.

"These guys just come," said Slim by way of introduction.

"Glad to meet ya," the big man said. "My name's Carlson."

"I'm George Milton. This here's Lennie Small," George said with a curt nod.

"Glad to meet ya. He ain't very small," Carlson said again and chuckled softly at his joke, repeating it to himself one more time under his breath. He turned to Slim and asked with a curious squint, "Meant to ask you, Slim – how's your bitch? I seen she wasn't under your wagon this mornin'."

"She slang her pups last night," said Slim. "Nine of them. Four of them got ate by Sick Ones right off. Smell of blood and placenta attracted them and ate them up."

"Got five left, huh?" Carlson said with a nod.

"Yeah, five. They were the biggest," Slim explained.

"What kinda dogs you think they're gonna be?" Carlson asked.

"I dunno," said Slim. "Some kinda huntin' dogs, I guess. That's the most kind I seen around here when she was in heat. Would be great to have some more back up around here."

Carlson went on, his questioning had an agenda, "Got five pups, huh. Gonna keep all of them?"

"I dunno. Have to keep them a while so they can drink Chip's milk," Slim replied thoughtfully.

Carlson said thoughtfully, "Well, look here, Slim. I been thinkin'. That dog of Candy's is so goddamn old he can't hardly walk. Stinks like hell, too. Every time he comes into the bunkhouse I can smell him for two, three days. Can't protect

Candy lettalone himself. Why don't you get Candy to shoot his old dog and give him one of the pups to raise up? I can smell that dog a mile away. Got no teeth, damn near blind, can't eat. Candy feeds him milk. He can't chew nothin' else."

George had been staring intently at Slim. Suddenly a triangle began to ring outside, slowly at first, and then faster and faster until the beat of it disappeared into one ringing sound. It stopped as suddenly as it had started.

"They're here," said Carlson without hesitation. Outside, there was a burst of voices as a group of men went by, gunshots sounded in the distance. Slim stood up slowly and with dignity and a calm determination.

"You guys better come while we're not overrun yet. Won't be no chance in a couple of minutes," Slim said matter-of-factly. Carlson stepped back to let Slim precede him, and then the two of them went out the door, guns in hand. Lennie was watching George excitedly. George rumpled his cards into a messy pile.

"Yeah!" George said, "I heard him, Lennie. I'll ask him."

"A brown and white one," Lennie cried excitedly.

"I said I'd ask," George said standing up. "Come on. Let's get out there. For now, we gotta worry about them Sick Ones."

Lennie didn't move from his bunk and said, "You ask him right away, George, so no more of them will get killed."

"Sure. Come on now, get up on your feet," George said with a sigh and retrieving his gun. Lennie rolled off his bunk and stood up, and the two of them started for the door. Just as they reached it, Curley bounced in.

"You seen a girl around here?" he demanded angrily. "About half an hour ago maybe." George said coldly, then added, "Better thin's to worry about though."

"Well, what the hell was she doin'?" Curley replied. He ignored, or simply didn't hear in his fury, the second statement. George stood still, watching the angry little man.

George said insultingly, "She said – she was lookin' for you."

Curley seemed really to see George for the first time. His eyes flashed over George, took in his height, measured his reach, looked at his trim middle … then saw the gun in his hand.

"Well, which way'd she go?" he demanded at last.

"I dunno," said George. "I didn't watch her go."

Curley scowled at him, then turned away and hurried out the door.

"George," Lennie said, panic in his voice.

George said, "Ya know, Lennie, I'm scared I'm gonna tangle with that bastard myself. I hate his guts. Jesus Christ! Come on. He worrin' about a tart and the ranch is swarmin'."

George readying his Luger and left, with Lennie lumbering behind.

The sunshine lay in a thin line under the window. From a distance, there could be heard the crack of gunshots. After a moment the ancient dog walked lamely in through the open door to find safety. He gazed about with mild, half-blind eyes. He sniffed, smelling that the room was free of decay that followed the Sick Ones, and then lay down and put his head between his paws. Curley popped into the doorway again and stood looking into the room. The dog raised his head, but when Curley jerked out, the grizzled head sank to the floor again.

CHAPTER 3

Although there was evening brightness showing through the windows of the bunkhouse, inside it was dusk. There loomed the ever-present smell of unnatural death in the air. Through the open door came the thuds and occasional clangs of a horseshoe game, and now and then the sound of voices raised in approval or derision. In the distance rang the occasional gunshot; whether they were from practice or defence was not known. Slim and George came into the darkening bunkhouse together and shut, without bolting, the heavy door. Slim reached up over the card table and turned on the tin-shaded electric light. Instantly the table was brilliant with light, and the cone of the shade threw its brightness straight downward, leaving the corners of the bunkhouse still in dusk. George felt apprehensive of the light and the Sick Ones natural draw to any signs of life such as the illumination, but the walls and door helped to dissuade the feeling. Slim sat down on a box and George took his place opposite.

"It was nothin'," said Slim. "I woulda had to drown some of them anyways, and the rest woulda just got ate eventually. No need to thank me about that."

George said, "It wasn't much to you, maybe, but it was a hell of a lot to him. Jesus Christ, I don't know how we're gonna get him to sleep in here. He'll wanta sleep right out in the barn with them. We'll have trouble keepin' him from gettin' right in the box with them pups."

"It was nothin'," Slim repeated. "Say, you sure was right about him. Maybe he ain't bright, but I never seen such a worker. He damn near tore two of the Sick Ones heads off like it won't nothin'. There ain't nobody can keep up with him. God almighty, I never seen such a strong guy. Didn't even need a gun."

George spoke proudly, "Just tell Lennie what to do and he'll do it if it don't take no figurin'. He can't think of nothin' to do himself, but he sure can take orders."

There was a crack of a revolver nearby outside and a little cheer of voices – whatever they shot at wasn't a threat any longer. Slim moved back slightly so the light was not on his face.

"Funny how you and him strin' along together," Slim said thoughtfully. It was Slim's calm invitation to confidence.

"What's funny about it?" George demanded, slightly defensive.

"Oh, I dunno. Hardly none of the guys ever travel together. I hardly never seen two guys travel together. You know how the world is, can't trust another guy on the road as much as you can trust the Sick Ones. Even workin' on the ranches, they just come in and get their bunk and remove some scalps, and then they quit and go out alone. Never seem to give a damn about nobody. It just seems kinda funny a cuckoo like him and a smart little guy like you travelin' together," Slim said. He didn't shrug, or even hedge his words – he was confident in what he said.

"He ain't no cuckoo He's dumb as hell, but he ain't crazy. And I ain't so bright neither, or I wouldn't be shootin' Sick Ones for my fifty and found. If I was bright, if I was even a little bit smart, I'd have my own little place, and I'd be payin' others to clear my own land, instead of doin' all the work and not worryin' about Sick Ones comin' out the ground for me," said George, gritting his teeth. Then, George fell silent. He wanted to talk. Slim neither encouraged nor discouraged him. He just sat back quiet and receptive. At last, George continued, "It ain't so funny, him and me goin' around together. Him and me was both born in Auburn. I knew this woman was tryna make him sick. She was sick herself. When she died, Lennie just come along with me out workin'. Got kinda used to each other after a little while."

"Hmm," said Slim, acknowledging the words of George. George looked over at Slim and saw the calm, godlike eyes fastened on him.

"Funny. I used to have a hell of a lot of fun with him. Used to play jokes on him 'cause he was too dumb to take care of himself. But he was too dumb even to know he had a joke played on him. I had fun. Made me seem goddamn smart alongside of him. Why he'd do any damn thin' I told him. If I told him to walk into a hoard of Sick Ones, over he'd go with open arms. That wasn't so damn much fun after a while. He never got mad about it, neither. I've beat the hell outta him, and he coulda bust every bone in my body just with his hands, but he never lifted a finger against me," George said, his voice was taking on the tone of confession. "Tell you what made me stop that. One day a bunch of guys was standin' around Sacramento when some Sick Ones showed up. I was feelin' pretty smart. I turns to Lennie and says, 'Chase them.' And he chases. Didn't realise they wouldn't run at the time. He damn near died before we could put them down. And he was so damn nice to me for savin' him. Clean forgot I told him to chase them to begin with. Well, I ain't done nothin' like that no more."

"He's a nice fella," said Slim. "Guy don't need no sense to be a nice fella. Seems to me sometimes it just works the other way around. Take a real smart guy and he ain't hardly ever a nice fella."

George stacked the scattered cards and began to lay out his solitaire hand. The shoes thudded on the ground outside. At the windows, the light of the evening still made the window squares bright.

"I ain't got no people," George said. "I seen the guys that go around on the ranches alone. That ain't no good. They don't have no fun. After a long time, they get mean. They get wantin' to fight all the time. Like a different kind of sickness sets in."

"Yeah, they get mean. They all go bad," Slim agreed. "They get so they don't wanta talk to nobody. Can't trust nobody. Don't wanna trust nobody."

"Course Lennie's a goddamn nuisance most of the time," said George with a smile, "but you get used to goin' around with a guy and you can't get rid of him."

"He ain't mean," said Slim. "I can see Lennie ain't a bit mean."

"Course he ain't mean. But he gets in trouble all the time 'cause he's so goddamn dumb. Like what happened in Monroeville–" He stopped talking and paused in the middle of turning over a card. He looked alarmed and peered over at Slim. George cursed himself for being lured into talking, but Slim had no judgement in his eyes. George asked conspiratorially, "You wouldn't tell nobody?"

"What'd he do in Monroeville?" Slim asked calmly.

"You wouldn't tell … no, course you wouldn't," George said, reassuring himself.

"What'd he do in Monroeville?" Slim asked again. He was still so calm, but insistent.

"Well, he seen this sick girl with red hair, except she wasn't completely sick just yet. She wasn't one of *them*. Dumb bastard like he is, he wants to touch everythin' he likes. Just wants to feel it. So he reaches out to feel this sick girls hair and the girl tries to bite him, and that gets Lennie all mixed up, and he holds on 'cause that's the only thin' he can think to do. Well, this girl gnashes and gnashes. I was just a little bit off, and I heard all the noise, so I comes runnin', and by that time Lennie's so scared all he can think to do is just hold on. I socked her over the head with a fence picket to put her down. He was so scared he couldn't leggo of that hair. And he's so goddamn strong, you know," George said, and began breathing heavily. He hadn't even realised, until he finished, that he told the story in one breath. He sighed and ran his hand through his hair. Slim's eyes were level and unwinking. He nodded very slowly.

"So, what happens?" Slim finally said, provoking George to continue. George carefully built his line of solitaire cards.

"Well, the town think Lennie's been bit. The guys in Monroeville start a party out to lynch Lennie so he can't spread the sickness. So we sit in an irrigation ditch underwater all the rest of that day. Got only our heads stickin' outta water, and up under the grass that sticks out from the side of the ditch. And that night we scrammed outta there," George admitted, a small weight being lifted off his shoulders by sharing *part* of his dark secret with Slim. Slim sat in silence for a moment.

Finally, Slim asked, "Didn't get bit though, huh?"

"Hell, no. He just got away," George lied, then added. "I can see why they think he was bit though – there was a lot of blood. I'd put him down myself if I thought he was. Besides, she hadn't fully turned at the time."

"He ain't got a fever," said Slim. "I can tell when someone is gonna be a Sick One a mile off."

"Course he don't, and he won't either. Like I said, he ain't bi–" George said before being cut off by Lennie coming through the door. He wore his blue denim coat over his shoulders like a cape, and he walked hunched way over. George said, changing his focus, "Hi, Lennie. How you like the pup now?"

Lennie said breathlessly, "He's brown and white just like I wanted."

He went directly to his bunk and lay down and turned his face to the wall and drew up his knees. George put down his cards very deliberately.

"Lennie," he said sharply.

Lennie twisted his neck, looked over his shoulder and said innocuously, "Huh? What you want, George?"

"I told you, you couldn't brin' that pup in here," George stated.

"What pup, George? I ain't got no pup," Lennie said, feigning innocence. George went quickly to him, grabbed him by the shoulder and rolled him over. He reached down and picked the tiny puppy from where Lennie had been concealing it against his stomach. Lennie sat up quickly.

"Give him to me, George," Lennie implored.

George said, "You get right up and take this pup back to the nest. He's gotta sleep with his mother. You wanta kill him? Just born last night and you take him out of the nest. You take him back or I'll tell Slim not to let you have him."

Lennie held out his hands pleadingly and begged, "Give him to me, George. I'll take him back. I didn't mean no harm, George. Honest I didn't. I just wanted to pet him a little."

George handed the puppy to him and urged him, "Alright. You get him back there quick, and don't you take him out no more. You'll kill him, the first thin' you know."

Lennie fairly scuttled out of the room. Slim had not moved. His calm eyes followed Lennie out the door.

"Jesus," Slim said, "he's just like a kid, ain't he?"

"Sure he's just like a kid. There ain't no more harm in him than a kid neither, except he's so strong. I bet he won't come in here to sleep tonight. He'd sleep right alongside that box in the barn. Well – let him. He ain't doin' no harm out there," George said in angry exasperation. Slim smiled and they both continued with their cards.

It was almost dark outside now. Old Candy, the Swamper, came in and went to his bunk, and behind him struggled his old dog.

"Hello, Slim. Hello, George. Didn't neither of you play horseshoes?" Candy asked politely.

"I don't like to play every night," said Slim. "Especially after the Sick Ones have been so active today."

Candy went on and asked with a grimace, "Either you guys got a slug of whisky? I gotta gut ache."

"I ain't," Slim said apologetically. "I'd drink it myself if I had, and I ain't got a gut ache neither."

"Gotta bad gut ache," Candy explained. "Them goddamn turnips give it to me. I knew they was goin' to before I ever ate them."

The thick-bodied Carlson came in out of the darkening yard. He walked to the other end of the bunkhouse and turned on the second shaded light.

"Darker than hell in here," he said. Then added with a smile, "Jesus, how that nigger can pitch shoes."

"He's plenty good," Slim agreed.

"Damn right he is. He don't give nobody else a chance to win—" said Carlson. He stopped and sniffed the air, and still sniffing, looked down at the old dog. He said in disgust, "God almighty, that dog stinks. Get him outta here, Candy! I don't never know if it's a Sick One or that old dog. You gotta get him out."

Candy rolled to the edge of his bunk. He reached over and patted the ancient dog.

Candy apologised, "I been around him so much I never notice how he stinks."

"Well, I can't stand him in here. That stink hangs around even after he's gone," said Carlson He walked over with his heavy-legged stride and looked down at the dog. "Got no teeth. He's all stiff with rheumatism. He ain't no good to you, Candy. He might even carry the Walkin' Plague, slowly makin' you a Sick One. Why don't you shoot him, Candy?"

The old man squirmed uncomfortably.

"Well – hell! I had him so long. Had him since he was a pup. I herded sheep with him," He said proudly. "You wouldn't think it to look at him now, but he was the best damn sheepdog I ever seen."

George said, "I seen a guy in Monroeville that had an Airedale that could herd sheep. Learned it from the other dogs."

Carlson was not to be put off.

"Look, Candy. This old dog just suffers hisself all the time. If you was to take him out and shoot him right in the back of the head—" he leaned over and pointed, "—right there, why he'd never know what hit him."

Candy looked about unhappily and said softly, "No. No, I couldn't do that. I had him too long."

"He don't have no fun," Carlson insisted, "and he stinks to beat hell. Tell you what. I'll shoot him for you. Then it won't be you that does it. Better than gettin' ate."

Candy threw his legs off his bunk. He scratched the white stubble whiskers on his cheek nervously.

"I'm so used to him," he said softly, almost pleading. "I had him from a pup."

"Well, you ain't bein' kind to him keepin' him alive," said Carlson. "Look, Slim's bitch got a litter right now. I bet Slim would give you one of them pups to raise up, wouldn't you, Slim?"

The skinner had been studying the old dog with his calm eyes.

"Yeah. You can have a pup if you wanta," Slim said. He seemed to shake himself free for speech. "Carl's right, Candy. That dog ain't no good to himself. I wish somebody would shoot me if I get old and a cripple."

Candy looked helplessly at him, for Slim's opinions were law.

"Maybe it'd hurt him," he suggested. "I don't mind takin' care of him."

"The way I'd shoot him, he wouldn't feel nothin'. I'd put the gun right there," Carlson said and pointed with his toe. "Right back of the head. He wouldn't even quiver."

Candy looked for help from face to face. It was quite dark outside by now. A young labouring man came in. His sloping shoulders were bent forward and he walked heavily on his heels, as though he moved an invisible corpse. He went to his bunk and put his hat on his shelf. Then he picked a pulp magazine from his shelf and brought it to the light over the table.

"Did I show you this, Slim?" he asked, not noticing the tension in the room.

"Show me what?" Slim asked, distracted from Candy and his dog. The young man turned to the back of the magazine, put it down on the table and pointed with his finger.

"Right there, read that. Go on," said the young man. Slim bent over it. The young man urged Slim, "Read it out loud."

"Ok Whit," Slim said and proceeded to read slowly. "'Dear Editor, I read your mag for six years and I think it is the best on the market. I like stories by Chesser and O'Brien. I think they are a whing-ding. Even give us more like Among the Dead. I don't write many letters. Just thought I'd tell you I think your mag is the best dime's worth I ever spent'."

Slim looked up questioningly and asked, "What you want me to read that for?"

Whit said, "Go on. Read the name at the bottom."

"'Yours for success, William Tenner'," He said and glanced up at Whit again. "What you want me to read that for?"

Whit closed the magazine impressively. "Don't you remember Bill Tenner? Worked here about three months ago?"

Slim thought for a moment and asked, "Little guy? Drove a cultivator? Used a pickaxe when it came to the Sick Ones?"

"That's him," Whit cried. "That's the guy!"

"You think he's the guy wrote this letter?" Slim asked.

"I know it. Bill and me was in here one day. Bill had one of them magazines that just come. He was lookin' in it and he says, 'I wrote a letter. Wonder if they put it in the magazine!' But it wasn't there. Bill says, 'Maybe they're savin' it for later.'

And that's just what they done. There it is," Whit replied excitedly.

"Guess you're right," said Slim. "Got it right in the magazine."

George held out his hand for the magazine. "Let's look at it?"

Whit found the place again, but he did not surrender his hold on it. He pointed out the letter with his forefinger, and then he went to his box shelf and laid the magazine carefully in.

"I wonder if Bill seen it," he said. "Bill and me worked in that patch of field peas. Run cultivators, both of us. Bill was a hell of a nice fella."

Carlson had refused to be drawn into the conversation. He continued to look down at the old dog. Candy watched him uneasily.

At last Carlson said, "If you want me to, I'll put the old devil out of his misery right now and get it over with. Ain't nothin' left for him. Can't eat, can't see, and can't even walk without hurtin'."

Candy said hopefully, "You ain't got no gun."

"The hell I ain't. Got a Luger. It won't hurt him none at all," Carlson said with annoyance.

Candy said desperately, "Maybe tomorrow. Let's wait till tomorrow."

"I don't see no reason for it," said Carlson. He went to his bunk, pulled his bag from underneath it and took out a Luger pistol. "Let's get it over with. We can't sleep with him stinkin' around in here."

He put the pistol in his hip pocket. Candy looked a long time at Slim to try to find some reversal. Slim gave him none.

At last, Candy said softly and hopelessly, "Alright – take him."

He did not look down at the dog at all. He lay back on his bunk and crossed his arms behind his head and stared at the ceiling. From his pocket, Carlson took a little leather thong. He stooped over and tied it around the old dog's neck. All the men except Candy watched him.

"Come boy. Come on, boy," he said gently. Then he said apologetically to Candy, "He won't even feel it."

Candy did not move nor answer him. Carlson twitched the thong.

"Come on, boy," Carlson said again. The old dog got slowly and stiffly to his feet and followed the gently pulling leash.

Slim said, "Carlson."

"Yeah?" Carlson said, turning momentarily.

"You know what to do," Slim said calmly with a nod.

"What you mean, Slim?" Carlson said, squinting his eyes at him.

"Take a shovel," said Slim shortly.

"Oh, sure! I get you," Carlson said, realisation lighting his face. He led the dog out into the darkness. George followed to the door and shut the door and set the latch gently in its place. Candy lay rigidly on his bed staring at the ceiling as the metal bar slid across.

Slim said loudly, "One of my lead mules got a bad hoof. Got to get some tar on it."

His voice trailed off. It was silent outside. Carlson's footsteps died away. The silence came into the room, and the silence lasted.

George chuckled, "I bet Lennie's right out there in the barn with his pup. He won't wanta come in here no more now he's got a pup."

Slim said, "Candy, you can have any one of them pups you want."

Candy did not answer. The silence fell on the room again. It came out of the night and invaded the room. All conversation felt forced, because it was, and could not dispel the crushing silence.

George asked the room, "Anybody like to play a little euchre?"

"I'll play out a few with you," said Whit.

They took places opposite each other at the table under the light, but George did not shuffle the cards. He rippled the edge of the deck nervously, and the little snapping noise drew the eyes of all the men in the room – so he stopped doing it. The silence fell on the room again. A minute passed, and another minute. Candy lay still, staring at the ceiling. Slim gazed at him for a moment and then looked down at his hands; he subdued one hand with the other, and held it down. There came a little gnawing sound from under the floor and all the men looked down toward it gratefully. Only Candy continued to stare at the ceiling.

"Sounds like there was a rat under there," said George, trying to fill the silence with something everyone knew. "We ought to get a trap down there."

"Fleas might spread the Walkin' Plague," Slim added. "Better safe than sorry."

Whit broke out, "What the hell's takin' him so long? Lay out some cards, why don't you? We ain't goin' to get no euchre played this way."

"Sure," George said with a nod and brought the cards together tightly, studying the backs of them. The silence was in the room again – it was almost tangible. A shot sounded in the distance. None of the men were strangers to gunshots, but that one laid heavily on all of their minds. The men looked quickly at the old man. Every head turned toward him. For a moment he continued to stare at the ceiling. Then he rolled slowly over and faced the wall and lay silent. George shuffled the cards noisily and dealt them. Whit drew a scoring board to him and set the pegs to start.

Whit said, "I guess you guys really come here to work."

"How do you mean?" George asked, curious by his words.

Whit laughed and explained, "Well, you come on a Friday. You got two days to work till Sunday."

"I don't see how you figure," said George puzzled.

Whit laughed again and said, "You do if you been around these big ranches much. Guy that wants to look over a ranch comes in Saturday afternoon. He gets Saturday night supper and three meals on Sunday, as well as safety and company, and he can quit Monday mornin' after breakfast without turnin' his hand. But you come to work Friday noon. You got to put in a day and a half no matter how you figure."

George looked at him levelly and said, "We're gonna stick around a while. Me and Lennie's gonna roll up a stake."

The door opened quietly and the stable buck put in his head; a lean negro head, lined with pain, the eyes patient.

"Mr Slim," he said politely. Slim took his eyes from old Candy.

No longer lost in thought, Slim replied, "Huh? Oh! Hello, Crooks. What's the matter?"

"You told me to warm up tar for that mule's foot. I got it warm," Crooks said politely.

"Oh! Sure, Crooks. I'll come right out and put it on," Slim replied coolly and thankfully.

"I can do it if you want, Mr Slim," Crooks added expectantly.

"No. I'll come do it myself," Slim said and nodded. He stood up.

Crooks said again, "Mr Slim."

"Yeah," Slim replied without any annoyance in his voice.

"That big new guy's messin' around with your pups out in the barn," Crooks explained uneasily.

"Well, he ain't doin' no harm. I give him one of them pups," Slim also explained with a nod.

"Just thought I'd tell ya," said Crooks. "He's takin' them outta the nest and handlin' them. That won't do them no good. If they die … the Sick Ones will smell it."

"He won't hurt them," said Slim. "I'll come along with you now."

George looked up and quipped, "If that crazy bastard's foolin' around too much, just kick him out, Slim."

Slim followed the stable buck out of the room. George dealt and Whit picked up his cards and examined them.

"Seen the new kid yet?" Whit asked.

"What kid?" George asked.

"Why, Curley's new wife," Whit said with a slight edge to his words.

"Yeah, I seen her," George said, doing his best to hide his distaste for her.

"Well, ain't she a looloo?" Whit asked, trying to draw George into his derogatory discussion.

"I ain't seen that much of her," said George, trying to avoid saying anything which could be used against him. Whit laid down his cards impressively.

"Well, stick around and keep your eyes open. You'll see plenty. She ain't concealin' nothin'. I never seen nobody like her. She got the eye goin' all the time on everybody. I bet she gives the stable buck the eye. I bet she'd even give a Sick One the eye too. I don't know what the hell she wants," Whit said with disgust.

George asked casually, "Been any trouble since she got here?"

It was obvious that Whit was not interested in his cards any longer. He laid his hand down and George scooped it in. George laid out his deliberate solitaire hand – seven cards, and six on top, and five on top of those.

Whit said, "I see what you mean. No, they ain't been nothin' yet. Curley's got yella-jackets in his drawers, but that's all so far. Every time the guys is around she shows up. She's lookin' for Curley, or she thought she left somethin' layin' around and she's lookin' for it. Seems like she can't keep away from guys. And Curley's pants is just crawlin' with ants, but they ain't nothin' come of it yet."

George said, "She's gonna make a mess. They're gonna be a bad mess about her. She's a jailbait all set on the trigger. That Curley got his work cut out for him. Ranch with a bunch of guys on it ain't no place for a girl, especially like her. It don't take much for men to turn on each other these days."

Whit said, "If you got ideas, you oughta come in town with us guys tomorrow night."

"Why? What's you doin'?" George asked suspiciously.

"Just the usual thin'. We go into old Susy's place. Hell of a nice place. Old Susy's a laugh – always crackin' jokes. Like she says when we come up on the front porch last Saturday night. Susy opens the door and then she yells over her shoulder, 'Get your guns, girls, here comes the Sick Ones', then she just bust out laughin'. She never talks dirty, neither. Got five girls there," Whit replied enthusiastically.

"What's it set you back?" George asked.

"Two and a half. You can get a shot for two bits. Susy got nice chairs to sit in, too. If a guy don't want a flop, why he can just sit in the chairs and have a couple or three shots and pass the time of day and Susy don't give a damn. She ain't rushin' guys through and kickin' them out if they don't want a flop," Whit warmly explained.

"Might go in and look the joint over," said George.

"Sure. Come along. It's a hell of a lot of fun – her crackin' jokes all the time. Like she says one time, she says, 'I've knew people that if they got a rag rug on the floor and a girl don't matter if they dead or livin' but think they're runnin' a parlour house.' That's Clara's house she's talkin' about. And Susy says, 'I know what you boys want,' she says. 'My girls is alive, and there ain't no water in my whisky,' she says. 'If any you guys wanta look at a kewpie doll lamp and take your own chance gettin' burned, why you know where to go.' And she says, 'There's guys around here walkin' dead 'cause they like to spend time with Clara's girls'," Whit said, a fleeting smile lifting the corners of his mouth now that he had George's attention.

George asked, "Clara runs the other house, huh?"

"Yeah," said Whit. "We don't never go there. Clara gets three bucks a crack and thirty-five cents a shot, and she don't crack no jokes. But Susy's place is clean and she got nice chairs. Don't let no goo-goos in, neither."

"But Clara's girls ain't really dead are they?" George asked with alarm.

"Course not," laughed Whit. "Just Susy crackin' a joke."

"Me and Lennie's rollin' up a stake," said George. "I might go in and sit and have a shot, but I ain't puttin' out no two and a half."

"Well, a guy got to have some fun sometime," said Whit. The door opened and Lennie and Carlson came in together. Lennie crept to his bunk and sat down, trying not to attract attention. Carlson reached under his bunk and brought out his bag. He didn't look at old Candy, who still faced the wall. Carlson found a little cleaning rod in the bag and a can of oil. He laid them on his bed and then brought out the pistol, took out the magazine and snapped the loaded shell from the chamber. Then he fell to cleaning the barrel with the little rod. When the ejector snapped, Candy turned over and looked for a moment at the gun before he turned back to the wall again.

Carlson said casually, "Curley been in yet?"

"No," said Whit. "What's eatin' on Curley?"

Carlson squinted down the barrel of his gun, "Lookin' for his old lady. I seen him goin' round and round outside."

Whit said sarcastically, "He spends half his time lookin' for her, and the rest of the time she's lookin' for him. Won't be surprised if she was givin' the eye to a couple of the Sick Ones."

Almost on cue, Curley burst into the room breathlessly and demanded, "Any you guys seen my wife?"

"She ain't been here," said Whit dismissively. Curley looked threateningly about the room.

"Where the hell's Slim?" Curley asked, barely holding his rage as his face transformed into a snarl.

"Went out in the barn," said George. "He was gonna put some tar on a split hoof."

Curley's shoulders dropped and squared. Regaining some composure, he asked, "How long ago'd he go?"

"Five, maybe ten, minutes," George said, not making eye contact with him, as if Curley were the least of his problems. Curley jumped out the door and banged it after him.

Whit stood up and said, "I guess maybe I'd like to see this. Curley's just spoilin' or he wouldn't start for Slim. And Curley's handy, goddamn handy. Best don't hope he gets his hands on a rifle or revolver. But just the same, he better leave Slim alone. Nobody don't know what Slim can do."

"Thinks Slim's with his wife, don't he?" said George with a little amusement in his voice.

"Looks like it," Whit said. "Course Slim ain't. Least I don't think Slim is. But I like to see the fuss if it comes off. Come on, let's go."

George said, "I'm stayin' right here. I don't wanta get mixed up in nothin'. Lennie and me got to make a stake."

Carlson finished the cleaning of the gun. He put the gun back in its holster on his hip, and the cleaning tools back in the bag and pushed the bag under his bunk.

"I guess I'll go out and look her over," he said. Old Candy lay still. Lennie, from his bunk, watched George cautiously. When Whit and Carlson were gone and the door closed after them, George turned to Lennie.

"What you got on your mind?" George hissed.

"I ain't done nothin', George. Slim says I better not pet them pups so much for a while. Slim says it ain't good for them; so I come right in. I been good, George," Lennie replied with a tone that suggested he was concerned that George didn't believe him.

"I coulda told you that," said George in disbelief.

"Well, I wasn't hurtin' them none. I just had mine in my lap pettin' it," Lennie said innocently and honestly.

George asked, "Did you see Slim out in the barn?"

"Sure I did. He told me I better not pet that pup no more," Lennie nodded.

"Did you see that girl?" George asked, almost like a parent trying to find out if their child had done something they weren't meant too.

"You mean Curley's girl?" Lennie answered innocently again.

"Yeah. Did she come in the barn?" George asked, his patience waning.

"No. Anyways I never seen her," Lennie said with a heavy shrug.

"You never seen Slim talkin' to her?" George asked again, pointing a finger at Lennie.

"Uh-uh. She ain't been in the barn," Lennie answered, not understanding what George was trying to get at.

"Okay," said George with relief. He added, "I guess them guys ain't gonna see no fight. If there's any fightin', Lennie, you keep out of it."

"I don't want no fights," said Lennie. He got up from his bunk and sat down at the table, across from George. Almost automatically George shuffled the cards and laid out his solitaire hand. He used a deliberate, thoughtful slowness. Lennie reached for a face card and studied it, then turned it upside down and studied it.

"Both ends the same," he said simply as if seeing them for the first time. "George, why is it both ends the same?"

"I don't know," said George. "That's just the way they make them. What was Slim doin' in the barn when you seen him?"

RYAN COLLEY

"Slim?" Lennie repeated.

"Sure. You seen him in the barn, and he told you not to pet the pups so much," George said, exasperation building again.

"Oh, yeah. He had a can of tar and a paint brush. I don't know what for," Lennie said, almost like he was counting off items on his fingers.

"You sure that girl didn't come in like she come in here today?" George said, beginning his line of questioning again.

"No. She never come," Lennie said definitively with a nod.

George sighed and said, looking at Lennie from the corner of his eye, "You give me a good whore house every time. A guy can go in and get drunk and get everythin' outta his system all at once, and no messes. And he knows how much it's gonna set him back. These here jailbaits ... you can trust the Sick Ones even more 'cause you know where you stand with them."

Lennie followed his words admiringly and moved his lips a little to keep up.

George continued, "You remember Franklin West, Lennie? Went to grammar school?"

"The one that his old lady used to make hotcakes for the kids?" Lennie asked dreamily.

"Yeah. That's the one. You can remember anythin' if there's anythin' to eat in it," George said rolling his eyes. George looked carefully at the solitaire hand. He put an ace up on his scoring rack and piled a two, three and four of diamonds on it. He added, almost as an afterthought, "Franklin's in San Savini right now on account of a tart."

Lennie drummed on the table with his fingers. He suddenly said, "George?"

"Huh?" George responded, Lennie pulling him from the deep thought he was about to enter.

"George, how long's it gonna be till we get that little place and live offa fatta the lan' – and rabbits?" Lennie asked eagerly.

"I don't know," said George. "We gotta get a big stake together. I know a little place we can get cheap, but they ain't givin' it away. Land around it is fulla Sick Ones, so that needs clearin' too."

Old Candy turned slowly over. His eyes were wide open. He watched George carefully.

Lennie said, "Tell about that place, George."

"I just told you, just last night," George sighed.

"Go on – tell again, George," Lennie said, a shine to eyes of childlike wonderment.

"Well, it's ten acres," said George, beginning his recital. "Got a little windmill. Got a little shack on it, and a chicken run. Got a kitchen, orchard, cherries, apples, peaches, apricots, nuts, got a few berries. A big wall. There's a place for alfalfa and plenty water to flood it. There's a pig pen—"

"And rabbits, George?" Lennie asked excitedly.

"No place for rabbits now, but I could easily build a few hutches and you could feed alfalfa to the rabbits," George said, allowing himself a small smile.

"Damn right, I could," said Lennie proudly. "You goddamn right I could."

George's hands stopped working with the cards. His voice was growing warmer.

"And we could have a few pigs. I could build a smokehouse like the one grandpa had, and when we kill a pig we can smoke the bacon and the hams, and make sausage and all like that. And when the salmon run up river we could catch a hundred of them and salt them down or smoke them. We could have them for breakfast. They ain't nothin' so nice as smoked salmon. When the fruit come in we could can it – and tomatoes, they're easy to can. Every Sunday we'd kill any Sick Ones hangin' round the area. Maybe we'd go into town and get shells to keep us safe. Apart from that, we keep ourselves goin'. Nothin' more, nothin' less," George said, the dream he had conjured almost tangible. Lennie watched him with wide eyes, and old Candy watched him too.

Lennie said softly, "We could live offa the fatta the lan'."

"Sure," said George. "All kinda vegetables in the garden, and if we want a little whisky we can sell a few eggs or kill a couple of Sick Ones for someone else. We'd just live there. We'd belong there. There wouldn't be no more runnin' round the country and gettin' fed by a Jap cook. No, sir, we'd have our own place where we belonged and not sleep in no bunkhouse."

"Tell about the house, George," Lennie begged.

"Sure, we'd have a little house and a room to ourselves. Little fat iron stove, and in the winter we'd keep a fire goin' in it. It ain't a lot of land so we wouldn't have to work too hard. Maybe six, seven hours a day. We wouldn't have to buck no barley eleven hours a day. And when we put in a crop, why, we'd be there to take the crop up. We'd know what come of our plantin'. And no bars on the window – the wall would keep us safe and we wouldn't be livin' in no prison," George said, imagining it almost as clearly as if it was in front of him.

"And rabbits," Lennie said eagerly. "And I'd take care of them. Tell how I'd do that, George."

"Sure, you'd go out in the alfalfa patch and you'd have a sack. You'd fill up the sack and brin' it in and put it in the rabbit cages," George said, allowing himself to be lost in the moment.

"They'd nibble and they'd nibble," said Lennie, "The way they do. I seen them."

"Every six weeks or so. They would throw a litter so we'd have plenty rabbits to eat and to sell. And we'd keep a few pigeons to go flyin' around the windmill like they done when I was a kid," George said. He looked raptly at the wall over Lennie's head before continuing, "and it would be our own, and nobody could can us. If we don't like a guy we can say, 'Get the hell out,' and by God he's got to do it. And if a friend come along, why we'd have an extra bunk, and we'd say, 'Why don't you spend the night?' and by God he would. We'd have a setter dog and a couple stripe cats, but you gotta watch out they don't carry no Walkin' Plague – it could drive them mad and attack the rabbits."

Lennie breathed hard and said quietly, "You just let them try to get the rabbits. I'll break their goddamn necks. I'll … I'll smash them with a stick."

He subsided, grumbling to himself, threatening any undead or sick animals which might dare to disturb the future rabbits.

George sat entranced with his own picture. When Candy spoke they both jumped as though they had been caught doing something reprehensible.

Candy said, "You know where a place is like that?"

George was on guard immediately.

"S'pose I do," he said. "What's that to you?"

"You don't need to tell me where it's at. Might be any place," old Candy shrugged.

"Sure," said George, glaring at him. "That's right. You couldn't find it in a hundred years."

Candy went on excitedly, "How much they want for a place like that?"

George watched him suspiciously before carefully saying, "Well – I could get it for six hundred bucks. The old people that owns it is flat bust and the old lady needs an operation. Say – what's it to you? You got nothin' to do with us."

"I ain't much good with only one hand. I lost my hand right here on this ranch. Slim cut it off when a Sick One bit me; stopped the spread. That's why they give me a job swampin'; plus people a little scared to come near me now. Think they might get sick too. And they give me two hundred and fifty dollars 'cause I lost my hand. And I got fifty more saved up right in the bank, right now. That's three hundred, and I got fifty more comin' the end of the month. Tell you what" Candy said and leaned forward eagerly. "S'pose I went in with you guys. That's three hundred and fifty bucks I'd put in. I ain't much good, but I could cook and tend the chickens and hoe the garden some. How'd that be?"

George half-closed his eyes and said thoughtfully, "I gotta think about that. We was always gonna do it by ourselves."

Candy interrupted him, "I'd make a will and leave my share to you guys in case I kick off, 'cause I ain't got no relatives nor nothin'. You guys got any money? Maybe we could do her right now?"

"We got ten bucks between us," George spat on the floor disgustedly, their dream so close yet so far. Then he said after a moment's consideration, "Look, if me and Lennie work a month and don't spend nothin', we'll have a hundred bucks. That'd be four fifty. I bet we could swin' her for that. Then you and Lennie could go get her started and I'd get a job and make up the rest, and you could sell eggs and stuff like that."

They fell into silence. They looked at one another, amazed. Smiles began to appear on their lips. This thing they had never really believed in was coming true.

"And the rabbits!" Lennie added excitedly with a huge grin.

"Jesus Christ! I bet we could swin' her," George continued reverently, his eyes were full of wonder. Then, he repeated softly to himself, "I bet we could swin' her."

The trio sat in silence as they thought about their dream becoming a reality. Candy sat on the edge of his bunk. He scratched the stump of his wrist nervously.

"I got hurt four year ago. They'll can me purty soon. Just as soon as I can't swamp out no bunkhouses they'll put me on the county. Maybe if I give you guys my money, you'll let me hoe in the garden even after I ain't no good at it. And I can help build a wall to keep us safe. But it'll be on our own place, and I'll be let to work on our own place," Candy said, and George nodded in agreement while still deep in thought. Candy continued miserably, "You seen what they done to my dog tonight? They says he wasn't no good to himself nor nobody else. When they can me here I wish somebody would shoot me. But they won't do nothin' like that. I won't have no place to go, and I can't get no more jobs. I'll be dead out there by weeks end. I'll have thirty dollars more comin', time you guys is ready to quit."

George sprung up in excitement and said, "We'll do her. We'll fix up that little old place and we'll go live there."

He sat down again. They all sat still, all bemused by the beauty of the thing, each mind was popped into the future when this lovely thing should come about.

"And the rabbits," Lennie insisted in a whisper to himself.

"S'pose they was a carnival or a circus come to town, or a ball game, or any damn thin'," George said wonderingly, after some time. Old Candy nodded in appreciation of the idea. George continued, "We'd just go to her. We wouldn't ask nobody if we could. Just say, 'We'll go to her,' and we would. Just milk the cow and slin' some grain to the chickens and go to her. Only shootin' Sick Ones that bothered us and not for others."

"And put some grass to the rabbits," Lennie broke in. "I wouldn't never forget to feed them. When we gonna do it, George?"

"In one month. Right squack in one month. Know what I'm gonna do? I'm gonna write to them old people that owns the place that we'll take it. And Candy'll send a hundred dollars to bind her," George said slapping his thigh at the lightbulb moment idea.

"Sure will," said Candy. "How they keepin' safe there at the moment?"

"Got a wooden fence round the whole place at the moment," George explained. "It ain't perfect, but does the job mostly. Won't take long to build it up."

"I'm gonna take my pup," said Lennie. "I bet by Christ he likes it there, by Jesus."

Voices were approaching from outside.

George said quickly, "Don't tell nobody about it. Just us three and nobody else. They liable to can us so we can't make no stake. Just go on like we was gonna shoot Sick Ones the rest of our lives, then all of a sudden someday we'll go get our pay and scram outta here."

Lennie and Candy nodded, and they were grinning with delight.

"Don't tell nobody," Lennie said to himself.

Candy said, "George."

"Huh?" George replied.

"I ought to of shot that dog myself, George. I shouldn't ought to have let no stranger shoot my dog," Candy said with regret. He looked up with tears in his eyes and said, "I shoulda took responsibility for it and done it myself."

The door opened. Slim came in, followed by Curley and Carlson and Whit. Slim's hands were black with tar and he was scowling. Curley hung close to his elbow.

Curley said, "Well, I didn't mean nothin', Slim. I just ask you."

"Well, you been askin' me too often. I'm gettin' goddamn sick of it. If you can't look after your own goddamn wife, what you expect me to do about it? You lay off of me," Slim said, never raising his voice once.

"I'm just tryna tell you I didn't mean nothin'," said Curley. "I just thought you might of seen her."

"Why don't you tell her to stay the hell home where she belongs?" said Carlson with a raised voice, whose anger had got the better of him. "You let her hang around bunkhouses and pretty soon you're gonna have somethin' on your hands and you won't be able to do nothin' about it."

Curley whirled on Carlson, sensing an easier target.

"You keep outta this unless you wanta step outside," Curley growled.

Carlson laughed, hand falling to his gun at his side, "You goddamn punk! You tried to throw a scare into Slim, and you couldn't make it stick. Slim threw a scare into you. You're yella as a frog belly. I don't care if you're the best welter in the country. You come for me, and I'll blow your goddamn head off."

Candy joined the attack with joy.

"Glove fulla vaseline," he said disgustedly. Curley glared at him, but his eyes slipped on past and lighted on Lennie. Lennie was still smiling with delight at the memory of his future home. Curley stepped over to Lennie like a terrier.

"What the hell you laughin' at?" Curley growled.

"Huh?" Lennie said looking up and blankly at him, unaware of what was unfolding around him. Then Curley's rage exploded.

"Come on, you big bastard. Get up on your feet. No big son-of-a-bitch is gonna laugh at me. I'll show you who's yella," Curley snarled, beginning to circle like a prowling cat. Lennie looked helplessly at George, and then he got up and tried to retreat. Curley was balanced and poised. He slashed at Lennie with his left, and then smashed down his nose with a right. Lennie gave a cry of terror. Blood welled from his nose. George saw the blood and began to panic – he was *sure* Lennie wasn't infected, as the sick girl hadn't completely turned when she bit him … but what if Lennie *was*? George watched Lennie's blood start to stream.

"George," he cried. "Make him leave me alone, George."

He backed away until he was against the wall, and Curley followed, slugging him in the face. Lennie's hands remained at his sides; he was too frightened to defend himself. Suddenly, worry for Lennie over rid his fear of Lennie's blood and George was on his feet.

"Get him, Lennie. Don't let him do it!" George yelled, feeling as though he almost shredded his vocal cords. Lennie covered his face with his huge paws and bleated with terror.

Lennie cried, "Make him stop, George."

Then Curley attacked his stomach and cut off his wind.

Slim jumped up and cried out, "The dirty little rat. I'll get him myself."

George put out his hand and grabbed Slim.

"Wait a minute," George said to Slim. He then cupped his hands around his mouth and yelled, "Get him, Lennie!"

Lennie took his hands away from his face and looked about for George, and Curley slashed at his eyes. The big face was covered with blood.

"He's gettin' beat," Slim said to George, preparing to move in to intervene. George looked at Slim, who stopped his movement and nodded.

George yelled again, "I said get him."

Curley's fist was swinging when Lennie reached for it. The next minute Curley was flopping like a fish on a line, and his closed fist was lost in Lennie's big hand. Lennie's blood splashed onto Curley's face and into his mouth, but Curley didn't react. George ran down the room. In that moment, everyone was silent.

"Leggo of him, Lennie. Leggo!" George called to Lennie but Lennie watched in terror the flopping little man whom he held. Blood ran down Lennie's face, one of his eyes was cut and closed. George slapped him in the face again and again, and still Lennie held on to the closed fist. Curley was white and shrunken by now, and his struggling had become weak. He stood crying, his fist lost in Lennie's paw.

"Ge-George!" Lennie called out, sobbing the word. George, ignoring Lennie's tears, shouted over and over.

"Leggo his hand, Lennie. Leggo. Slim, come help me while the guy got any hand left," George said desperately. Suddenly Lennie let go his hold. He crouched cowering against the wall.

"You told me to, George," he said miserably. Curley sat down on the floor, looking in shocked wonder at his crushed hand. Slim and Carlson bent over him. Then Slim straightened up and regarded Lennie with horror.

"We got to get him to a doctor," he said. "Looks to me like every bone in his hand is bust."

"I didn't wanta," Lennie cried. "I didn't wanta hurt him."

Slim said, "Carlson, you get the wagon hitched up. We'll take him into Soledad and get him fixed up. I need someone else to be our shooter."

Carlson hurried out, quickly followed by Whit holding a rifle. Slim turned to the whimpering Lennie, all horror gone from his face.

"It ain't your fault," Slim said. "This punk sure had it comin' to him. But – Jesus! He ain't hardly got no hand left."

Slim hurried out, and in a moment returned with a tin cup of water. He held it to Curley's lips. Curley sipped, wetting his dry mouth and unknowingly swallowed the splash of Lennie's blood that had landed on his lips in the struggle. George thought beyond Curley and more of himself, the way men often do when they feel endangered.

George whispered to Slim, "Slim, will we get canned now? We need the stake. Will Curley's old man can us now?"

Slim smiled wryly. He knelt down beside Curley.

"You got your senses in hand enough to listen?" he asked. Curley nodded. Slim went on, "Well, then listen. I think you got your hand caught in a machine. If you don't tell nobody what happened, we ain't goin' to. But you just tell and try to get this guy canned and we'll tell everybody, and then you won't get the last laugh."

"I won't tell," said Curley, his voice barely a whisper. He avoided looking at Lennie. George fell back and breathed a sigh of relief. He looked at Candy who nodded back to him, George sat down and waited the eternity that it felt for the wagon.

Buggy wheels sounded outside. Slim helped Curley up.

"Come on now. Carlson's gonna take you to a doctor," Slim said as he helped Curley out the door. The sound of wheels drew away. In a moment Slim came back into the bunkhouse. He looked at Lennie, still crouched fearfully against the wall.

"Let's see your hands," he asked. Lennie stuck out his hands. Slim looked at it and eyes widened. "Christ almighty, I hate to have you mad at me."

George broke in and explained, "Lennie was just scared. He didn't know what to do. I told you nobody ought never to fight him … No, I guess it was Candy I told."

Candy nodded solemnly and said, "That's just what you done. Right this mornin' when Curley first lit into your friend, you says, 'He better not fool with Lennie if he knows what's good for him.' That's just what you says to me."

George turned to Lennie and said, "It ain't your fault. You don't need to be scared no more. You done just what I told you to. Maybe you better go in the washroom and clean up your face. You look like hell."

Lennie smiled with his bruised mouth and split lips.

"I didn't want no trouble," he said. He walked toward the door, but just before he came to it, he turned back. "George?"

"What you want?" George sighed, suddenly tired.

"I can still tend the rabbits, George?" Lennie asked hopefully.

"Sure. You ain't done nothin' wrong," George said and smiled.

"I didn't mean no harm, George," Lennie said again to make sure George knew.

"Well, get the hell out and wash your face," George said, his smile fading as he watched Lennie leave.

CHAPTER 4

Crooks, the black stable buck, had his bunk in the harness room; a little shed that leaned off the wall of the barn. On one side of the little room there was a square four-paned window, and on the other, a narrow plank door leading into the barn. Crooks' bunk was a long box filled with straw, on which his blankets were flung. On the wall by the window there were pegs on which hung broken harness in process of being mended, strips of new leather, and under the window itself a little bench for leather-working tools, curved knives and needles and balls of linen thread, and a small hand riveter. On pegs were also pieces of harness, a split collar with the horsehair stuffing sticking out, a broken hame, and a trace chain with its leather covering split. It wasn't Crooks' room, where supplies were also kept. It was a storeroom, where Crooks' had been allowed to sleep. Not an inch of that room was truly his as it could just as easily be repurposed by someone else if the need arose. Most importantly, the room wasn't safe. There weren't any bars on the window, nor a latch on the door to keep Crooks' safe. There were no true weapons for someone to defend themselves with unless they got creative in their hour of need or, like Crooks' had done, brought one in with them. The lock on the door didn't work half the time. To sleep in the harness room was to be truly vulnerable.

Crooks had his apple box over his bunk and in it a range of medicine bottles – both for himself and for the horses. There were cans of saddle soap and a drippy can of tar with its paintbrush sticking over the edge. Scattered about the floor were a number of personal possessions because, as Crooks told himself to justify it, he was alone and he could leave his things about without fear of someone taking them. Also being a stable buck and a cripple, he was more permanent than the other men, and he had accumulated more possessions than he could carry on his back. Crooks possessed several pairs of shoes, a pair of rubber boots, a big alarm clock and a single-barrelled shotgun which Crooks had repaired from parts found or discarded. He had books, too; a tattered medical text and a mauled copy of human anatomy concerning the undead from the previous year. There were battered magazines concerning the Walking Plague and the undead, and a few dirty books on a special shelf over his bunk. A pair of large gold-rimmed spectacles hung from a nail on the wall above his bed. This room was swept and fairly neat, for Crooks was a proud, aloof man. He kept his distance and demanded that other people keep theirs. His body was bent over to the left by his crooked spine. His eyes lay deep in his head and, because of their depth, seemed to glitter with intensity. His lean face was lined with deep black wrinkles, and he had thin, pain-tightened lips which were lighter than his face.

It was Saturday night. Through the open door that led into the barn came the sound of moving horses, of feet stirring, of teeth champing on hay, of the rattle of halter chains. In the stable buck's room, a small electric globe threw a meagre yellow light. Crooks sat on his bunk. His shirt was out of his jeans in back. In one hand he held a bottle of liniment and, with the other, he rubbed his spine. Now and then he poured a few drops of the liniment into his pink-palmed hand and reached up under his shirt to rub again. He flexed his muscles against his back and shivered.

Noiselessly Lennie appeared in the open doorway and stood there looking in, his big shoulders nearly filling the opening. For a moment Crooks did not see him, but on raising his eyes he stiffened, his hand came out from under his shirt and he dived for his shotgun before realising it was Lennie and not one of the undead. A scowl came on his face. Lennie smiled helplessly in an attempt to make friends.

Crooks said sharply, "You got no right to come in my room. This here's my room. Nobody got any right in here but me."

Lennie gulped and his smile grew more fawning, he explained, "I ain't doin' nothin'. Just come to look at my puppy. And I seen your light."

"Well, I got a right to have a light. You go on and get outta my room. I ain't wanted in the bunkhouse, and you ain't wanted in my room," Crooks said, shooing Lennie away.

"Why ain't you wanted?" Lennie asked innocently.

"'Cause I'm black. They play cards in there, but I can't play 'cause I'm black. They say I stink. Well, I tell you, you all of you stink to me," Crooks spat. Lennie flapped his big hands helplessly.

"Everybody went into town," he said. "Slim and George and everybody. George says I gotta stay here and not get in no trouble. I seen your light."

"Well, what do you want?" Crooks asked in irritation.

"Nothin' – I seen your light. I thought I could just come in and sit," Lennie asked hopefully. Crooks stared at Lennie, and he reached behind him and took down the spectacles and adjusted them over his pink ears and stared again.

"I don't know what you're doin' in the barn anyway," Crooks complained. He continued by way of an explanation. "You ain't no skinner. There's no call for a bucker or a shooter to come into the barn at all. You ain't no skinner. You ain't got nothin' to do with the horses … and you hadn't rung the bell, so Sick Ones ain't attackin'."

"The pup," Lennie repeated obliviously. "I come to see my pup."

"Well, go see your pup, then. Don't come in a place where you're not wanted," Crooks tutted. Lennie lost his smile. He advanced a step into the room, then remembered and backed to the door again.

"I looked at them a little. Slim says I ain't to pet them very much," Lennie explained.

Crooks said, "Well, you been takin' them out of the nest all the time. I wonder the old lady don't move them someplace else."

"Oh, she don't care. She lets me," Lennie said. He had moved into the room again. Crooks scowled, but Lennie's disarming smile defeated him.

"Come on in and sit a while. Long as you won't get out and leave me alone, you might as well sit down," Crooks said. His tone was a little friendlier. "All the boys gone into town, huh?"

"All but old Candy. He just sets in the bunkhouse sharpenin' his pencil and sharpenin' and figurin'," Lennie said dishearteningly.

Crooks adjusted his glasses and asked quizzically, "Figurin'? What's Candy figuring' about?"

Lennie almost shouted, "About the rabbits!"

"You're nuts," said Crooks, shaking his head. "You're crazy as a wedge. What rabbits you talkin' about?"

"The rabbits we're gonna get, and I get to tend them, cut grass and give them water, and like that," Lennie explained ecstatically.

"Just nuts," Crooks reiterated. "I don't blame the guy you travel with for keepin' you outta sight."

Lennie said quietly, "It ain't no lie. We're gonna do it. Gonna get a little place and live offa fatta the lan'."

Crooks settled himself more comfortably on his bunk.

"Sit down," he invited. "Sit down on the nail keg."

Lennie hunched down on the little barrel.

"You think it's a lie," Lennie said. "But it ain't no lie. Every word's the truth, and you can ask George."

Crooks put his dark chin into his pink palm.

"You travel around with George, don't ya?" Crooks asked.

"Sure. Me and him goes every place together," Lennie said, again, with excitement.

"Sometimes he talks, and you don't know what the hell he's talkin' about. Ain't that so?" Crooks continued. He leaned forward, boring into Lennie with his deep eyes. "Ain't that so?"

"Yeah," Lennie admitted slowly.

"Just talks on, and you don't know what the hell it's all about?" Crooks continued, eyes narrowing.

"Yeah ... sometimes. But ... not always," Lennie nodded.

Crooks leaned forward over the edge of the bunk and said, "I ain't a southern Negro. I was born right here in California. My old man had a chicken ranch, about ten acres. The white kids come to play at our place, and sometimes I went to play with them, and some of them was pretty nice. My old man didn't like that. I never knew till long later why he didn't like that. But I know now."

"Oh," Lennie said simply without any real meaning behind the word. At the very least, he didn't understand what Crooks meant.

"There wasn't another coloured family for miles around. And now there ain't a coloured man on this ranch and there's just one family in Soledad," Crooks said after some hesitation but when he had spoken his voice was softer. He added with a laugh, "If I say somethin', why it's just a nigger sayin' it."

Lennie asked, "How long you think it'll be before them pups will be old enough to pet?"

"A guy can talk to you and be sure you won't go blabbin'. Couple of weeks and them pups will be all right. George knows what he's about. Just talks and you don't understand nothin'," Crooks laughed again. He leaned forward excitedly. "This is just a nigger talkin', and a busted-back nigger. So it don't mean nothin', see? You couldn't remember it anyways. I seen it over and over – a guy talkin' to another guy and it don't make no difference if he don't hear or understand. The thin' is, they're talkin', or they're sittin' still not talkin'. It don't make no difference, no difference."

Lennie just looked at him quizzically, nodding but not understanding.

"Uh-huh," Lennie said, still nodding but looking confused. Crooks excitement had increased until he pounded his knee with this hand.

"George can tell you screwy thin's, and it don't matter. It's just the talkin'. It's just bein' with another guy. That's all," Crooks continued before he paused. His voice grew soft and persuasive. "S'pose George don't come back no more. S'pose he got bit and just ain't comin' back. What'll you do then?"

Lennie's attention came gradually to what had been said like a creeping darkness.

"What?" he demanded.

"I said s'pose George went into town tonight and he got ate by one of the Sick Ones," Crooks whispered conspiratorially and pressed forward some kind of private victory. He repeated, "Just s'pose that."

"He won't let it happen. George is smart and protects me. I been with George a long a time. He'll come back tonight!" Lennie cried, but the doubt was too much for him. Full of fear, he asked, "Don't you think he will?"

Crooks' face lighted with pleasure in his torture and he observed calmly, "Nobody can't tell what a guy will do. Let's say he wants to come back and can't. S'pose he does come back and he's a Sick One too. We'll have to put him down."

Lennie struggled to understand and said desperately, "George is still George. Even if he's a Sick One. He still George. George is careful. He won't get hurt. He ain't never been hurt, 'cause he's careful."

"Well, s'pose, just s'pose he don't come back. What'll you do then?" Crooks taunted. Lennie's face wrinkled with apprehension.

"I don' know. Say, what you doin' anyways?" Lennie cried out angrily. "This ain't true. George ain't got hurt."
Crooks bored in on him, sensing George as Lennie's weakness. "Want me to tell you what will happen? They'll take you to the booby hatch. They'll tie you up with a collar, like a Sick One on show," Crooks threatened maliciously. Suddenly Lennie's eyes centred and grew quiet, and mad. He stood up and walked dangerously toward Crooks.

"Who hurt George?" Lennie savagely demanded. Crooks saw the danger as it approached him. He edged back on his bunk to get out of the way.

"I was just supposin'," he said meekly. "George ain't hurt. He's all right. He'll be back all right."

Lennie stood over him. "What you supposin' for? Ain't nobody goin' to suppose no hurt to George."

Crooks removed his glasses and wiped his eyes with his fingers.

"Just sit down," Crooks said gently, as if trying to pacify a wild beast. "George ain't hurt."

Lennie growled back to his seat on the nail keg and grumbled, "Ain't nobody goin' to talk no hurt to George."

Crooks soothed, "Maybe you can see now. You got George. You know he's goin' to come back. S'pose you didn't have nobody. S'pose you couldn't go into the bunkhouse and play rummy 'cause you was black. How'd you like that? S'pose you had to sit out here and read books. Sure you could play horseshoes till it got dark, but then you got to read books. Books ain't no good. A guy needs somebody. Somebody to be near him. A guy goes nuts if he ain't got nobody. Don't make no difference who the guy is, long as he's with you. I tell ya. I tell you a guy gets too lonely and he gets sick."

"George gonna come back," Lennie reassured himself in a frightened voice. "Maybe George come back already. Maybe I better go see."

"I didn't mean to scare you," Crooks said filled with regret. "He'll come back. I was talkin' about myself. A guy sits alone out here at night, maybe readin' books or thinkin' or stuff like that. Sometimes he gets thinkin', and he got no one to tell him what's so and what ain't so. Maybe if he sees somethin', he don't know whether it's right or not. He can't turn to some other guy and ask him if he sees it too. He can't tell. He got nothin' to measure by. I seen thin's out here. I wasn't drunk. I don't know if I was asleep. Thought the Sick

Ones eatin' other men in the night was in my mind to begin with. No one to ask! If some guy was with me, he could tell me I was asleep, and then it would be all right. But I just don't know."

Crooks was looking across the room now, looking toward the window.

Lennie sniffed miserably, "George wouldn't go away and leave me. I know George wouldn't do that."

The stable buck went on dreamily, "I remember when I was a little kid on my old man's chicken ranch. Had two brothers. They was always near me, always there. Used to sleep right in the same room, right in the same bed – all three. Had a strawberry patch. Had an alfalfa patch. Used to turn the chickens out in the alfalfa on a sunny mornin'. My brothers would sit on a fence rail and watch them – white chickens they was."

Gradually Lennie's interest came around to what was being discussed again and said simply, "George says we're gonna have alfalfa for the rabbits."

"What rabbits?" Crooks asked with genuine interest this time.

"We're gonna have rabbits and a berry patch," Lennie repeated.

"You're nuts," Crooks said shaking his head with a small smile.

"We are too. You ask George," Lennie said defensively.

"You're nuts," Crooks said scornfully, suddenly losing any interest in humouring Lennie. He went on, "I seen hundreds of men come by on the road and on the ranches, with their bindles on their back. They all think they got land out there somewhere. They think the sickness will go soon; like everythin' will be normal again. And that same damn thin' in their heads. Hundreds of them. They come, and they quit and go on if they lucky, or they die here 'cause of the Walkin' Plague – and every damn one of them got a little piece of land in his head where they safe. And never a goddamn one of them ever gets it. Just like heaven. Everybody wants a little piece of land. I read plenty of books out here. Nobody never gets to heaven, and nobody gets no land. It's just in their head. They're all the time talkin' about it, but it's just in their head."

He paused and looked toward the open door, for the horses were moving restlessly and the halter chains clinked. A horse whinnied.

"What's that?" Lennie asked nervously.

"I guess somebody's out there … or maybe *somethin'*," Crooks said anxiously. "Maybe Slim. Slim comes in sometimes two, three times a night. Slim's a real skinner. He looks out for his team."

He pulled himself painfully upright and moved toward the door. Then, just as suddenly as it began, the horses were silent. Unnaturally silent. No horses. No chains. Crooks reached for his shotgun with a nervous hand.

"What's is it?" Lennie asked again.

"Shh," Crooks hushed Lennie, and then called, "That you, Slim?"

After a few moments, Candy's voice answered, "Slim went in town. Say, you seen Lennie?"

All the tension in the harness shed dispersed, Crooks breathed out when he realised he was holding his breath and leaned his shotgun against the wall.

"Ya mean the big guy?" Crooks asked in return, opening the door which never quite closed.

"Yeah. Seen him around any place?" Candy called back.

"He's in here," Crooks said shortly. He went back to his bunk and lay down.

Candy stood in the doorway scratching his bald wrist and looking blindly into the lit room. He made no attempt to enter.

"Tell you what, Lennie. I been figurin' out about them rabbits," Candy began, ignoring Crooks now that Lennie was his focus.

Crooks said irritably, "You can come in if you want."

Candy seemed embarrassed and said awkwardly, "I don't know. Course, if you want me to."

"Come on in. If everybody's comin' in, you might just as well." Crooks asked, feigning annoyance, but a smile tugging at the corners of his mouth. It was difficult for Crooks to conceal his pleasure with anger. Candy came in, but he was still embarrassed.

"You got a nice cosy little place in here," he said to Crooks. "Must be nice to have a room all to yourself this way."

"Sure," said Crooks sourly, "and a manure pile under the window. Sure, it's swell."

Lennie broke in eagerly, cutting off Crooks, "You said about them rabbits."

Candy leaned against the wall beside the broken collar while he scratched the wrist stump.

"I been here a long time," he said looking around, "and Crooks been here a long time. This is the first time I ever been in his room."

Crooks said darkly, "Guys don't come into a coloured man's room very much. Nobody been here but Slim. Slim and the Boss."

Candy quickly changed the subject sensing potential hostility and said, "Slim's as good a skinner as I ever seen."

Lennie leaned toward the old Swamper.

"About them rabbits," Lennie insisted. Candy smiled.

"I got it figured out. We can make some money on them rabbits if we go about it right," Candy began, remembering what he'd been working out.

"But I get to tend them," Lennie broke in, a combination of not understanding and not caring about the specifics. "George says I get to tend them. He promised."

Crooks interrupted brutally, "You guys is just kiddin' yourself. You'll talk about it a hell of a lot, but you won't get no land. You'll be a Swamper here till they take you out in a box or blow out your brains. Hell, I seen too many guys. Lennie here'll quit and be on the road in two, three weeks. Seems like every guy got land in his head."

Candy rubbed his cheek angrily and spat, "You goddamn right we're gonna do it. George says we are. We got the money right now."

"Yeah?" said Crooks with a laugh. "Where's George now? In town in a whore house. That's where your money's goin'. Jesus, I seen it happen too many times. I seen too many guys with land in their head. They never get none under their hand."

Candy cried out defensively, "Sure they all want it. Everybody wants a little bit of land, not much. Just somethin' that was his. Somethin' he could live on and be safe! I never had none. I planted crops for damn near everybody in this state, but they wasn't my crops, and when I harvested them, it wasn't none of my harvest. But we gonna do it now, and don't you make no mistake about that. George ain't got the money in town. That money's in the bank. Me and Lennie and George. We gonna have a room to ourself. We're gonna have a dog and rabbits and chickens. We're gonna have green corn and maybe a cow or a goat."

When Candy stopped, overwhelmed by his own picture, Crooks asked, "You say you got the money?"

"Damn right. We got most of it. Just a little bit more to get. Have it all in one month. George got the land all picked out, too," Candy said proudly.

"I never seen a guy really do it. I seen guys nearly crazy with loneliness for land, but every time a whore house or a blackjack game took what it takes," Crooks said as he reached around and explored his spine with his hand. He hesitated before adding, while trying to force any hope down that he felt, "If ... if you ... guys would want a hand to work for nothin' – just his keep, why I'd come and lend a hand. I ain't so crippled I can't work like a son-of-a-bitch if I wanta. I could even collect bounty on a few Sick Ones I'd kill and add money to it too."

"Any you boys seen Curley?" asked a female voice. They swung their heads toward the door. Looking in was Curley's wife. Her face was heavily made up. Her lips were slightly parted. She breathed strongly, as though she had been running.

"Curley ain't been here," Candy said sourly. She stood still in the doorway, smiling a little at them, rubbing the nails of one hand with the thumb and forefinger of the other. Her eyes travelled from one face to another.

"They left all the weak ones here," she said finally. "Think I don't know where they all went? Even Curley. I know where they all went."

Lennie watched her, fascinated, but Candy and Crooks were scowling down away from her eyes.

Candy said, "Then if you know, why you wanta ask us where Curley is at?"

She regarded them amusedly.

"Funny thin'. If I catch any one man, and he's alone, I get along fine with him. But just let two of the guys get together and you won't talk. Just nothin' but mad," she said, biting her lip playfully. She dropped her fingers and put her hands on her hips. "You're all scared of each other, that's what. Every one of you is scared the rest is goin' to get somethin' on you."

After a pause Crooks said, "Maybe you better go along to your own house now. We don't want no trouble."

"Well, I ain't givin' you no trouble. Think I don't like to talk to somebody every once in a while? Think I like to stick in that house all the time?" Curley's wife blurted out angrily. Candy laid the stump of his wrist on his knee and rubbed it gently with his hand.

Candy said accusingly, "You got a husband. You got no call foolin' around with other guys, causin' trouble."

"Sure I got a husband. You all seen him. Swell guy, ain't he? Spends all his time sayin' what he's gonna do to guys he don't like, and he don't like nobody. If there no one to dislike, he says about all the Sick Ones he gonna kill. Think I'm gonna stay in that two-by-four house and listen how Curley's gonna lead a resistance of the livin' against the ones with the Walkin' Plague? 'Just one shot to the head' he says. 'Just one shot and they'll go down for good'," she said, flaring up with rage. Then she paused and her face lost its sullenness and grew interested. "Say – what happened to Curley's hand?"

There was an embarrassed silence. Candy stole a look at Lennie. Then he coughed.

"Why … Curley … he got his hand caught in a machine, ma'am. Bust his hand," Candy muttered, avoiding eye contact with Candy's wife. She watched for a moment, and then she laughed.

"Baloney! What you think you're sellin' me? Curley started somethin' he didn't finish. Caught in a machine – baloney! Why, he ain't give nobody the good old one-two since he got his hand bust. Who bust him?" she said looking at them all one by one.

Candy repeated sullenly, "Got it caught in a machine."

"Alright. Alright, cover him up if you wanta. What do I care? You bindle bums think you're so damn good. What do you think I am, a kid? I tell you I coulda been nice and safe with a real hunter. Not even have to go outside. And a guy told me he could keep me safe for life …" she said contemptuously but stopped when she was breathless with indignation. "Saturday night. Everybody out doin' somethin'. Everybody! And what am I doin'? Standin' here talkin' to a bunch of bindlestiffs – a nigger and a dumb-dumb and a lousy old sheep – and likin' it 'cause they ain't nobody else."

Lennie watched her, his mouth half-open. Crooks had retired into the terrible protective dignity that he held as a black man. But a change came over old Candy. He stood up suddenly and knocked his nail keg over backwards.

"I had enough," he said angrily. "You ain't wanted here. We told you, you ain't. And I tell ya, you got floozy ideas about what us guys amounts to. You ain't got sense enough in that chicken head to even see that we ain't stiffs. S'pose you get us canned. S'pose you do. You think we'll hit the highway and get ate on the road. You don't know that we got our own ranch to go to, and our own house. We ain't got to stay here. We got a house and chickens and a damn wall to keep us safe at night. And we got friends, that's what we got. Maybe there was a time when we was scared of gettin' canned, but we ain't no more. We got our own land, and it's ours, and we can go to it."

Curley's wife laughed at him and said, "Baloney. I seen too many you guys. If you had two bits in the world, why you'd be in gettin' two shots of corn with it and suckin' the bottom of the glass. I know you guys."

Candy's face had grown redder and redder, but before she was done speaking, he had control of himself. He was the master of the situation.

"I might of knew," he said gently. "Maybe you just better go along and try to flatter a Sick One or two – least they'd actually want you. They'd want you for your face and body. We ain't got nothin' to say to you at all. We know what we got, and we don't care whether you know it or not. So maybe you better just scatter along now, 'cause Curley maybe ain't gonna like his wife out in the barn with us bindle stiffs."

She looked from one face to another, and they were all closed against her. Finally, she looked longest at Lennie, until he dropped his eyes in embarrassment.

Suddenly she said, "Where'd you get them bruises on your face?"

Lennie looked up guiltily and asked, "Who? Me?"

"Yeah, you," Curley's wife said, pushing for an answer. Lennie looked to Candy for help, and then he looked at his lap again.

"He got his hand caught in a machine," he said in shame.

Curley's wife laughed and said knowingly, "Okay, Machine. I'll talk to you later. I like machines."

Candy broke in angrily, "You leave this guy alone. Don't you do no messin' around with him. I'm gonna tell George what you says. George won't have you messin' with Lennie."

"Who's George?" she asked with a squint. "The little guy you come with?"

Lennie smiled happily and said, "That's him. That's the guy, and he's gonna let me tend the rabbits."

"Well, if that's all you want, I might get a couple rabbits myself," Curley's wife said coyly. Crooks stood up from his bunk and faced her.

"I had enough," he said coldly. "You got no rights comin' in a coloured man's room. You got no rights messin' around in here at all. Now you just get out and get out quick. If you don't, I'm gonna ask the Boss not to ever let you come in the barn no more."

She turned on him in scorn and said, her voice full of malice, "Listen, Nigger. You know what I can do to you if you open your trap?"

Crooks stared hopelessly at her, and then he sat down on his bunk and drew into himself.

She closed on him, not giving an inch, "You know what I could do?"

Crooks seemed to grow smaller, and he pressed himself against the wall.

"Yes, ma'am," he said weakly.

"Well, you keep your place then, Nigger. I could get you taken out, tied to a tree and we'd laugh as the Sick Ones ate you so easy it ain't even funny," she said with a wicked and evil smile. Crooks had reduced himself to nothing. There was no personality, no ego – nothing to arouse either like or dislike. In some ways, he was like one of the undead – a shell of who he had once been.

He said, and his voice was toneless, "Yes, ma'am."

For a moment she stood over him as though waiting for him to move so that she could whip at him again, but Crooks sat perfectly still, his eyes averted, everything that might be hurt drawn in. She turned at last to the other two. Old Candy was watching her, fascinated, the same way people would a horrific tragedy taking place.

"If you was to do that, we'd tell," he said quietly. "We'd tell about you framin' Crooks."

"Tell and be damned," she cried. "Nobody would listen to you, and you know it. Nobody would listen to you."

Candy subsided and agreed, "No … nobody would listen to us."

Lennie whined, "I wish George was here. I wish George was here."

"Don't you worry none. I just heard the guys comin' in. George will be in the bunkhouse right now, I bet," Candy stepped over to him and comforted him. He turned to Curley's wife and said quietly, "You better go home now. If you go right now, we won't tell Curley you was here."

She appraised him cooly. "I ain't sure you heard nothin'."

"Better not take no chances," he said cooly. "If you ain't sure, you better take the safe way."

She turned to Lennie and said with a small smile, "I'm glad you bust up Curley a little bit. He had it comin' to him. Sometimes I'd like to bust him myself."

She slipped out the door and disappeared into the dark barn. While she went through the barn, the halter chains rattled, and some horses snorted and some stamped their feet. Crooks seemed to come slowly out of the layers of protection he had put on.

"Was that the truth what you said about the guys come back?" he asked.

"Sure. I heard them," Candy said, not entirely certain himself.

"Well, I didn't hear nothin'," Crooks said dismissively.

"The gate banged," Candy said, and he went on, "Jesus Christ, Curley's wife can move quiet. I guess she had a lot of practice, though. Much rather a Sick One creep on me than her though."

"Maybe you guys better go," Crooks said, he avoided the whole subject now. "I ain't sure I want you in here no more. A coloured man got to have some rights even if he don't like them."

Candy said, "That bitch didn't ought to of said that to you."

"It wasn't nothin'," Crooks said dully. "You guys comin' in and sittin' made me forget. What she says is true – I ain't no better than the Sick Ones."

The horses snorted out in the barn and the chains rang and a voice called, "Lennie. Oh, Lennie. You in the barn?"

"It's George," Lennie cried, and he answered George, "Here, George. I'm right in here."

In a second George stood framed in the door, and he looked disapprovingly about and said, "What you doin' in Crooks' room? You shouldn't be here."

Crooks nodded, "I told them, but they come in anyways."

"Well, why don't you kick them out?" George questioned, not viciously, but for Crooks own sake.

"I didn't care much," said Crooks. "Lennie's a nice fella."

Now Candy aroused himself and said excitedly, "Oh, George! I been figurin' and figurin'. I got it worked out how we can even make some money on them rabbits."

George scowled. "I thought I told you not to tell nobody about that."

Candy was crestfallen and said dejectedly, "Didn't tell nobody but Crooks."

George said, "Well you guys get outta here. Jesus, seems like I can't go away for a minute."

Candy and Lennie stood up and went toward the door.

Crooks called, "Candy!"

"Huh?" Candy responded.

"Remember what I said about hoein' and doin' odd jobs?" Crooks asked sadly.

"Yeah," said Candy. "I remember."

"Well, just forget it," said Crooks, remembering his perceived place. "I didn't mean it. Just foolin'. I wouldn't wanta go no place like that."

"Well … okay, if you feel like that. Good night," Candy said with a nod. The three men went out of the door. As they went through the barn the horses snorted and the halter chains rattled. Crooks sat on his bunk and looked at the door for a moment, and then he reached for the liniment bottle. He pulled out his shirt in back, poured a little liniment in his pink palm and, reaching around, he fell slowly to rubbing his back.

CHAPTER 5

One end of the great barn was piled high with new hay and stabbed deeply into the pile was a pitchfork, its handle worn smooth and shiny from the work of many hands over the years. The hay came down like a mountain slope to the other end of the barn, and there was a level place as yet unfilled with the new crop. At the sides the feeding racks were visible and, between the slats, the heads of horses could be seen. It was Sunday afternoon. The resting horses nibbled the remaining wisps of hay, and they stamped their feet and they bit the wood of the mangers and rattled the halter chains; they sensed something was amiss. The afternoon sun sliced in through the cracks of the barn walls and lay in bright lines on the hay. There was the buzz of flies in the air, the lazy afternoon humming. From outside came the clang of horseshoes on the playing peg and the shouts of men, playing, encouraging, and jeering. However, in the barn, it was quiet and humming and lazy and warm. Only Lennie was in the barn, and he sat in the hay beside a packing case under a manger in the end of the barn that had not been filled with hay. Lennie sat in the hay, with a heavy sheen of sweat on his skin, and looked at a little dead puppy that lay in front of him. Lennie looked at it for a long time, and then he put out his huge hand and stroked it, stroked it clear from one end to the other.

"Why do you got to get killed? You ain't so little as mice. I didn't bounce you hard," Lennie said softly to the puppy. He bent the puppy's head up and looked in its face, and he said to it, "Now maybe George ain't gonna let me tend no rabbits if he finds out you got killed."

He scooped a little hollow and laid the puppy in it and covered it over with hay, out of sight, but he continued to stare at the mound he had made.

He said, "This ain't no bad thin' like I got to go hide in the brush. Oh no. This ain't. I'll tell George I found it dead."

He unburied the puppy and inspected it, and he stroked it from ears to tail.

Lennie continued on sorrowfully to himself, "But he'll know. George always knows. He'll say, 'You done it. Don't try to put nothin' over on me.' And he'll say, 'Now just for that you don't get to tend no rabbits!'"

Lennie continued to unbury the puppy. Suddenly his anger arose.

"Goddamn you," he cried. "Why do you got to get killed? You ain't so little as thumbs. You shouldn't break so easy!"

He picked up the puppy and hurled it from him. He turned his back on it.

He sat bent over his knees and he whispered, "Now I won't get to tend the rabbits. Now he won't let me."

He rocked himself back and forth in his sorrow.

From outside came the clang of horseshoes on the iron stake, and then a little chorus of cries. Lennie got up and brought the puppy back and laid it on the hay and sat down. He stroked the puppy again.

"You wasn't big enough. They told me and told me you wasn't. I didn't know you'd get killed so easy," he said with sorrow. He worked his fingers on the puppy's limp ear tenderly.

"Maybe George won't care. This here goddamn little son-of-a-bitch wasn't nothin' to George."

Curley's wife came around the end of the last stall. She came very quietly and Lennie didn't hear her. She wore her bright cotton dress and the mules with the red ostrich feathers. Her face was made-up and the little sausage curls were all in place. She was quite near to him before Lennie looked up and saw her. In a panic, he shovelled hay over the puppy with his fingers. He looked sullenly up at her.

She asked quizzically, "What you got there, sonny boy?"

Lennie glared at her and said, "George says I ain't to have nothin' to do with you – talk to you or nothin'."

"George givin' you orders about everythin'?" she laughed.

Lennie looked down at the hay and whispered, "Says I can't tend no rabbits if I talk to you or anythin'."

"He's scared Curley will get mad. Well, Curley got his arm in a slin', and if Curley gets tough, you can break his other hand. You didn't put nothin' over on me about gettin' it caught in no machine," she said quietly, but Lennie was not to be drawn in.

"No, sir. I ain't gonna talk to you or nothin'," he said anxiously. She knelt gently in the hay beside him.

"Listen," she said softly, "all the guys got a horseshoe tournament goin' on. It's only about four o'clock. None of them guys is goin' to leave that tournament. Why can't I talk to you? I never get to talk to nobody. I get awful lonely."

Lennie said belligerently, "Well, I ain't supposed to talk to you or nothin'."

"I get lonely," she repeated, then continued desperately, "You can talk to people, but I can't talk to nobody but Curley. Else he gets mad. How'd you like not to talk to anybody?"

"Well, I ain't supposed to. George's scared I'll get in trouble," Lennie said, refusing to listen.

She changed the subject and asked, "What you got covered up there?"

Then all of Lennie's woe came back on him and he said sadly, "Just my pup. Just my poor little pup."

Lennie swept the hay from on top of it.

"Why is he – oh, he's dead!" she cried in alarm, leaning away – fear of anything dead a newly created instinct.

"He was so little," said Lennie quietly. "I was just playin' with him ... and he made like he's gonna bite me ... and I made like I was gonna smack him ... and ... and I done it. And then he was dead!"

She leaned in slowly, and cautiously at first, but when his eyes began to fill with tears she couldn't help but console him.

"Don't you worry none. He was just a mutt. You can get another one easy. The whole country is fulla mutts," she said sympathetically and smiled.

"It ain't that so much," Lennie explained miserably. "George ain't gonna let me tend no rabbits now."

"Why don't he?" Curley's wife huffed with annoyance over Lennie's plight.

"Well, he said if I done any more bad thin's he ain't gonna let me tend the rabbits," Lennie said sourly.

She moved closer to him and she spoke soothingly, "Don't you worry about talkin' to me. Listen to the guys yell out there. They got four dollars bet in that tournament. None of them ain't gonna leave till it's over!"

"If George sees me talkin' to you he'll give me hell," Lennie said cautiously. "He told me so."

Her face grew angry.

"What's the matter with me?" she cried desperately. "Ain't I got a right to talk to nobody? What do they think I am, anyways? You're a nice guy. I don't know why I can't talk to you. I ain't doin' no harm to you."

"Well, George says you'll get us in a mess," Lennie explained and tutted, trying to avoid eye contact.

"Aw, nuts! What kinda harm am I doin' to you? Seems like they ain't none of them cares how I gotta live. The dead is walkin' and I married a little angry man! I coulda made somethin' of myself," she said and added darkly, "Maybe I will yet."

"Huh?" Lennie asked, struggling to focus on the meaning of her words. Suddenly, her words tumbled out in a passion of communication as though she hurried before her listener could be taken away.

"I lived right in Salinas," she began, and continued as if her very existence depended on it. "Come there when I was a kid and lived there until I married Curley. One day, a group of men come through town, and I met one of them. They were huntin' the Sick Ones – lookin' for people before they'd turned. He says I could go with them and he'd protect me. But my old lady wouldn't let me. She says 'cause I needed to marry. But the guy says I coulda. If I'd went, I wouldn't be livin' like this, you bet."

Lennie stroked the puppy back and forth. In response, he explained, "We gonna have a little place, and rabbits."

"Another time I met a guy, and he was a doctor. Went out to the Willamette Mercy Hospital with him. He says he was gonna show me where the Sick Ones come from. Says he knew

I wasn't afraid. Said I'd make a great nurse. Soon as he got back to Monroeville he was gonna write to me about it," she went on with her story quickly, before she could be interrupted and looked closely at Lennie to see whether she was impressing him. She continued, "I never got that letter. I always thought my old lady stole it. Well, I wasn't gonna stay no place where I couldn't get nowhere or make somethin' of myself, and where they stole your letters, I ask her if she stole it, too, and she says no. So I married Curley. Met him when he was tryin' to get the attention of them hunters. Thought he'd join them."

"Mm," Lennie said, still stroking the dead puppy.

When she saw Lennie's eyes were on the dead puppy, she demanded, "You listenin'?"

"Me? Sure," Lennie nodded.

"Well, I ain't told this to nobody before. Maybe I ought not to. I don't like Curley. He ain't a nice fella," she said sadly and, because she had confided in him, she moved closer to Lennie and sat fully beside him. "Coulda been kept safe by a real hunter, or even help save the world as a nurse. Been looked after, or been able to look after myself. And I coulda sat in a big mansion and had pictures took of me. And when the Walkin' Plague finished, and people stopped gettin' sick and the dead stopped walkin' … well, I coulda said to hell with everyone 'cause I'd been safe and happy, 'cause the hunter woulda helped. Or I woulda helped people in the hospital and people woulda thanked me. 'Cause this guy says I was a natural."

She looked up at Lennie, she took his arm gently and pretended to inject him an invisible syringe before smiling warmly to show that she could have been a great nurse. Lennie rubbed the spot where she had pretended to inject him, as if he had felt a prick, and sighed deeply. From outside came the clang of a horseshoe on metal, and then a chorus of cheers.

"Somebody made a ringer," said Curley's wife. Now the light was lifting as the sun went down, and the sun streaks climbed up the wall and fell over the feeding racks and over the heads of the horses.

Lennie said, "Maybe if I took this pup out and threw him away George wouldn't never know. And then I could tend the rabbits without no trouble."

Curley's wife said angrily, "Don't you think of nothin' but rabbits?"

"We gonna have a little place," Lennie explained patiently. "We gonna have a house and a garden and a place for alfalfa, and that alfalfa is for the rabbits, and I take a sack and get it all fulla alfalfa and then I take it to the rabbits."

She asked curiously, "What makes you so nuts about rabbits?"

Lennie had to think carefully before he could come to a conclusion. He moved cautiously close to her, until he was right against her.

"I like to pet nice thin's. Once at a fair I seen some of them long-hair rabbits. And they was nice, you bet. Sometimes I've even pet thumbs, but not when I couldn't get nothin' better," Lennie explained with a faraway look in his eyes.

Curley's wife moved away from him a little, not quite understanding what he meant by "thumbs" but still wary, and said, "I think you're nuts."

"No I ain't," Lennie explained earnestly. "George says I ain't. I like to pet nice thin's with my fingers, soft thin's."

She was a little bit reassured, and said with a smile, "Well, who don't? Everybody likes that. I like to feel silk and velvet. Do you like to feel velvet?"

Lennie chuckled with pleasure and cried out happily, "You bet, by God! And I had some, too. A lady give me some, and that lady – she become a Sick One. She give it right to me – about this big a piece. I wish I had that velvet right now."

"Where is it?" she asked quietly, happy to have someone to talk too. A frown came over his face.

"I lost it," he admitted. He looked up at her sadly and said, "I ain't seen it for a long time."

"You're nuts … but you're a kinda nice fella. Just like a big baby. But a person can see kinda what you mean. When I'm doin' my hair sometimes I just sit and stroke it 'cause it's so soft," Curley's wife laughed, a little bit at Lennie and a little bit at herself. Then, to show how she did it, she ran her fingers over the top of her head and Lennie watched patiently. She continued complacently, "Some people got kinda coarse hair. Take Curley. His hair is just like wire – prolly from the blood he always gettin' in it. But mine is soft and fine. 'Cause I brush it a lot. That makes it fine. Here – feel right here."

She took Lennie's hand and put it on her head.

"Oh," Lennie said automatically when he felt how soft it was. "This is a lot softer than thumbs."

"Feel right around there and see how soft it is," she said and smiled. She was happy for the physical human contact, not in a romantic way but in a platonic one. Lennie's big fingers fell to stroking her hair and she warned him, "Don't, you'll mess it up!"

"Oh! That's nice!" Lennie exclaimed ecstatically, and he stroked harder. "Oh, that's nice."

"Look out now! You'll mess it up! You stop it now, you'll mess it all up!" She cried out angrily. Lennie stroked harder and harder, she jerked her head sideways, and his fingers closed on her hair reflexively and hung on tightly. She continued crying out, not in anger but in panic, "Leggo! You leggo!"

The panic in the voice of Curley's wife was mirrored in Lennie. His face was contorted. She screamed, and Lennie's other hand closed heavily over her mouth and nose.

"Please don't," he begged, his fear evident in his voice. "Oh! Please don't do that. George will be mad."

She struggled violently under his hands. Her feet battered on the hay. She thrashed and struggled. She writhed to be free, and from under Lennie's hand came a muffled scream.

"Leggo!" she managed to scream through his huge hands. Lennie began to cry with fright.

"Oh! Please don't do none of that," he begged desperately. "George gonna say I done a bad thin'. He ain't gonna let me tend no rabbits!"

"Hel—" she began to scream out. He moved his hand tighter against her mouth and she bit him hard. Her teeth cut into his skin, only the smallest of cuts, and a jet of blood flew into her mouth and down her throat. Then Lennie grew angry.

"Now don't. I don't want you to yell. You gonna get me in trouble just like George says you will. Now don't you do that," he said like an angry parent, and she continued to struggle, and her eyes were wide and wild with terror. He shook her then, and demanded, "Don't you go yellin'."

He shook her violently, and her body flopped like a fish, and Lennie continued to bleed into her mouth. Then, as suddenly as it all began, she was still for Lennie had broken her neck. He looked down at her, and carefully he removed his bloody hand from over her mouth, and she lay still.

"I don't wanta hurt you, but George will be mad if you yell," he said cautiously. When she didn't answer, nor move, he bent closely over her. He lifted her arm and let it drop. For a moment he seemed bewildered. Then he whispered in fright, "I done a bad thin'. I done another bad thin'."

He pawed up the hay until it partly covered her. From outside the barn came a cry of men and the double clang of shoes on metal. For the first time, Lennie became conscious of the outside. He crouched down in the hay and listened.

"I done a real bad thin'," he said, thinking aloud. "I shouldn't of did that. George will be mad. And ... he said ... and hide in the brush ... till he come. He's gonna be mad. In the brush till he come. Don't go near no Sick Ones and hide in the brush. That's what he said."

Lennie went back and looked at the dead girl. The puppy lay close to her. Lennie picked it up in his giant hands.

"I'll throw him away," he said, thinking hard. "It's bad enough as it is."

He put the puppy under his coat, and he crept to the barn wall and peered out between the cracks, toward the horseshoe game. Then he crept around the end of the last manger and disappeared.

The sun streaks were high on the wall by now, and the light was growing soft in the barn. Curley's wife lay on her back, and she was half-covered with yellow hay. Then, with that, all the meanness and the planning and the discontent and the ache for attention were all gone from her face. She was very pretty and simple, and her face was sweet and young. Now her rouged cheeks and her reddened lips made her seem alive and sleeping very lightly. The curls, tiny little sausages, were spread on the hay behind her head, and her lips were parted. It was very quiet in the barn, and the quiet of the afternoon was on the ranch. Even the clang of the pitched shoes, even the voices of the men in the game, seemed to grow more quiet. The air in the barn was dusky in advance of the outside day. A pigeon flew in through the open hay door and circled and flew out again. Around the last stall came a shepherd bitch, lean and long, with heavy, hanging dugs. Halfway to the packing box where the puppies were, she caught the dead scent of Curley's wife, and the hair arose along her spine. She whimpered and cringed to the packing box. She began to move among the puppies, as if to settle, but something unnatural in the air spooked her and she left without her young. Then, as happens sometimes, a moment settled and hovered and remained for much more than a moment. The sound stopped and movement stopped for much, much more than a moment. Then gradually time awakened again and moved sluggishly on. The horses stamped on the other side of the feeding racks and the halter-chains clinked. Outside, the men's voices became louder and clearer. From around the end of the last stall, old Candy's voice came.

"Lennie! Oh, Lennie! You in here? I been figurin' some more. Tell you what we can do, Lennie. Oh, Lennie!" old Candy called as he appeared around the end of the last stall, and then he stopped and his body stiffened when he saw Curley's wife. He rubbed his smooth wrist on his white stubble whiskers. "I didn't know you was here."

Suddenly, Curley's wife's eyes flew open and she slowly sat up, as if an unseen puppeteer worked her body from the heavens. The movement was awkward and unnatural, yet Candy didn't seem to notice the strange and irregularly animated movement, nor did he notice the glassy look in her eyes. When she didn't answer, he stepped nearer.

"You ought not to sleep out here," he said disapprovingly, and then he was beside her when she lunged at him and snarled. He moved back and cried out, "Oh, Jesus Christ!"

He looked about helplessly, and he rubbed his beard as he backed away. Then he went quickly out of the barn and bolted it from the outside, but the barn was alive now. The horses stamped and snorted, and they chewed the straw of their bedding and they clashed the chains of their halters. The undead Curley's wife took note of the other living creatures trapped with her and made her way towards them. Her jaw and red lips hung slack as she swayed and stumbled, fixated on the flesh of the puppies.

In a moment Candy came back, and George was with him.

George said, "What was it you wanted to see me about?"

Candy pointed at the barn. George stared at it.

"What is it?" he asked. He stepped closer and opened it. At first, he saw nothing. He crept in slowly and saw the walking corpse that was Curley's wife. Then he echoed Candy's words. "Oh, Jesus Christ!"

He reached for the Luger he normally kept with him, only to remember it was in the bunkhouse. She turned towards the commotion, forgetting the last of the puppies momentarily. George's eyes fell to the puppies that Curley's wife was now done with, their discarded carcasses all that was left of their innocent and tiny bodies. The shambling corpse then turned around and revealed her bloodstained lips, a different shade of red than they had always been previously. She began to make her way towards him. George then acted, himself being puppeteered by instinct as opposed to logic. He swiped one of the pitchforks from the side of the barn and charged at her. He was not able to bring it to head level in the short distance, the only sure way to end the second life of the undead. Instead, he aimed at her chest. He made contact, piercing and tearing the flesh, but he didn't stop. He pushed and pushed until her back connected with the far side of the barn. The prongs of the pitchfork had run through her chest and out the other side of her slender body, pinning her to the wooden barn wall. Fresh blood fell from the holes in her breast, and also from the ones in her back, but that did not stop her cawing and clawing for him. Even in death, her seductive nature was clear. George moved, slowly and stiffly, his face was as hard and tight as wood, and his eyes were hard.

Candy said, "What done it?"

"Ain't you got any idea?" George asked and looked coldly at him.

Candy was silent for a long time before he slowly asked, "Lennie was bit wasn't he."

George said hopelessly, "I guess no one just gets the Walkin' Plague like that. Aint no Sick Ones about and Lennie is gone."

Candy asked desperately, "What we gonna do now, George? What we gonna do now?"

George was a long time in answering, longer even than Candy.

Slowly, he said exactly what he thought was going to happen, "Guess … we gotta tell the … guys. I guess we gotta get him and lock him up. We can't let him get away. Why, the poor bastard would starve. Maybe they'll lock him up and be nice to him."

Candy interrupted with a strange dreaded excitement, "We oughta let him get away. You don't know that Curley. Curley gonna wanta get him lynched. Curley will get him killed. If he got the Walkin' Plague anyway … it's only a matter of time."

George watched Candy's lips carefully, as if that would bring him a better understanding.

He sighed and said at last, "Yeah, that's right, Curley will. And the other guys will. Ain't no justice like mob justice anymore."

He looked back at Curley's wife who still reached for them, then Candy spoke his greatest fear.

"You and me can get that little place, can't we, George? You and me can go there and live nice, can't we? Can't we?" Candy begged. Before George answered, Candy dropped his head and looked down at the hay. He knew.

George said softly, "I think I knew from the very first. I think I knew we'd never do it. He used to like to hear about it so much I got to thinkin' maybe we would."

"Then ... it's all off?" Candy asked sulkily.

George didn't answer his question, but instead said, "I'll work my month and I'll take my fifty bucks and I'll stay all night in some lousy cat house. Or I'll sit in some poolroom till everybody goes home. And then I'll come back and work another month and I'll have fifty bucks more. Maybe, if I'm lucky, I'll pass out drunk and get ate by the Sick Ones."

Candy said, without hearing George, "He's such a nice fella. I didn't think he'd do nothin' like this."

"Lennie never done it in meanness. All the time he done bad thin's, but he never done one of them mean," George said, still staring at Curley's wife. He straightened up and looked back at Candy. "He for sure didn't mean to kill her ... and he prolly didn't even know he could make her sick ... now listen. We gotta tell the guys. They got to brin' him in, I guess. They ain't no way out. Maybe they won't hurt him. I ain't gonna let them hurt Lennie. Now you listen. The guys might think I was in on it. I'm gonna go in the bunkhouse. Then in a minute you come out and tell the guys about her, and I'll come along and make like I never seen her. Will you do that? So the guys won't think I was in on it?"

Candy said, "Sure, George. Sure I'll do that."

"Okay. Give me a couple minutes then, and you come runnin' out and tell like you just found her. I'm goin' now," George said calmly. George turned and went quickly out of the barn. Old Candy watched him go. He looked helplessly back at Curley's wife, and gradually his sorrow and his anger grew into words.

"You goddamn tramp. You done it, didn't you? I s'pose you're glad. Everybody knew you'd mess thin's up. You wasn't no good. You ain't no good now, you lousy undead tart!" he said viciously before he snivelled, and added with a shaky voice, "I coulda hoed in the garden and washed dishes for them guys."

Candy paused, spying the pitchfork penetrating her chest; an obvious sign of their presence. He approached Curley's wife and gripped the fork handle with his one remaining hand. She continued to reach hungrily for him.

Candy went on in a singsong and he repeated the old words, "If they was a circus or a baseball game … we woulda went to her … just said 'To hell with work,' and went to her. Never ask nobody's say so. And they'd of been a pig and chickens … and in the winter … the little fat stove … and the rain comin' … and us just sittin' there."

His eyes blinded with tears and wiped them away with his wrist stump. With that, he yanked the pitchfork out of the barn side wall and from Curley's wife. She snarled and tried to follow but was slow in her footwear. He turned and went weakly out of the barn, bolted the barn and he rubbed his bristly whiskers with his wrist stump. He tossed the pitchfork out of sight; he had to just hope no one saw, or took notice of, the wounds it had caused. Candy sighed, thinking about his words. No matter the venom in his words, she didn't hear them, and even if she could comprehend them it wouldn't have mattered. Curley's wife was no longer in the body that once belonged to her. Candy composed himself and approached the men.

Outside the noise of the game stopped. There was a rise of voices in question, a drum of running feet and the men burst into the barn. Slim, Carlson, Whit, Curley, and Crooks all kept back out of grabbing range. Candy came after them, and last of all came George. George had put on his blue denim coat and buttoned it, and his black hat was pulled down low over his eyes. The men raced around the last stall. Their eyes found Curley's wife in the gloom, they stopped and stood still and looked. Although she just stood there swaying, she managed to appear a lot more animated with the sight of potential food. Then Slim went quietly over to her, and he slipped a blade through her eye and destroyed her brain. One lean finger touched her cheek sadly, and then his hand went to her side and held her. He lowered her to the floor, gently and tenderly. Her body remained unmoving, as it should be after death. His hands slipped under her slightly twisted neck and his fingers explored it. When he stood up the men crowded near and the spell was broken. Curley came suddenly to life.

"I know who done it. That big son-of-a-bitch done it. I know he done it. Why … everybody else was out there playin' horseshoes," he cried and worked himself into a fury. "I'm gonna get him. I'm goin' for one of the guns. I'll kill the big son-of-a-bitch myself. I'll shoot him in the guts. Come on, you guys."

He ran furiously out of the barn.

"I'll get my Luger," Carlson said and he ran out too.

"I guess Lennie done it, all right. Her neck's bust. Lennie coulda did that," Slim said quietly to George. George didn't answer, but he nodded slowly. His hat was so far down on his forehead that his eyes were covered. Slim went on, "He was bit wasn't he, at that time in Monroeville you was tellin' about."

Again George nodded.

Slim sighed, "Well, I guess we got to get him. Where you think he might of went?"

It seemed to take George some time to free his words.

"He ... woulda went south," he said at last. "We come from north so he woulda went south."

"I guess we gotta get him," Slim repeated. George stepped close.

"Couldn't we maybe brin' him in and they'll lock him up? He's nuts, Slim. He never done this to be mean," George asked desperately clutching at straws.

Slim nodded and said, "We might. If we could keep Curley in, we might. But Curley's gonna wanta shoot him. Curley's still mad about his hand. And s'pose they lock him up and strap him down and put him in a cage. That ain't no good, George. He'll turn eventually anyway."

"I know," said George with a dawning realisation. "I know."

Carlson came running in and shouted, "The bastard stole my Luger. It ain't in my bag. George, I got your Luger for you too."

Curley followed him, and Curley carried a rifle in his good hand. Curley was cold now.

"All right, you guys," he said, like a commander rallying the soldiers. "The nigger's got a shotgun. You take it, Carlson. When you see him, don't give him no chance. Shoot for his guts. That'll double him over."

Whit said adrenalised, "I ain't got a gun."

"You go in Soledad and get a cop. Get Richard Grimes, he's deputy sheriff. Let's go now," Curley said. He turned suspiciously on George. "You're comin' with us, fella."

"Yeah," said George. Then he tried to explain, as he had nothing to lose. "I'll come. But listen, Curley. The poor bastard is nuts. Don't shoot him. He didn't know what he was doin'."

"Don't shoot him?" Curley cried out, not in sadness but disbelief that someone would deny him his revenge. "He got Carlson's Luger and the plague in his blood. Course we'll shoot him."

George said weakly, "Maybe Carlson lost his gun."

"I seen it this mornin'," said Carlson, shaking his head. "No, it's been took."

Slim stood looking down at Curley's wife and said, "Curley ... maybe you better stay here with your wife."

Curley's face reddened and he said, "I'm goin'. I'm gonna shoot the guts outta that big bastard myself, even if I only got one hand. I'm gonna get him."

Slim turned to Candy and said, "You stay here with her then, Candy. The rest of us better get goin'."

They moved away. George stopped a moment beside Candy and they both looked down at the dead girl until Curley called after him.

"George! You stick with us so we don't think you had nothin' to do with this," came Curley's voice, full of malice. George moved slowly after them, and his feet dragged heavily. Then they were gone, Candy squatted down in the hay and watched the face of Curley's wife.

"Poor bastard," he said softly. The sound of the men grew fainter. The barn was darkening gradually and, in their stalls, the horses shifted their feet and rattled the halter-chains.

119

Old Candy lay down in the hay and covered his eyes with his arm. Tears fell unimpeded.

CHAPTER 6

The deep green pool of the Salinas River was still in the late afternoon. Already the sun had left the valley to go climbing up the slopes of the Gabilan Mountains, and the hilltops were rosy in the sun. By the pool, among the mottled sycamores and beyond sight of those with the Walking Plague, a pleasant shade had fallen.

A water snake glided smoothly up the pool, twisting its periscope head from side to side, and it swam the length of the water and came to the legs of a motionless heron that stood in the shallows. A silent head and beak lanced down and plucked it out by the head, and the beak swallowed the little snake while its tail waved frantically. For once, the undead could not be seen or heard. A far rush of wind sounded and a gust drove through the tops of the trees like a wave, carrying a foul stench that reminded the living that the threat to humanity still loomed. The sycamore leaves turned up their silver sides, the brown, dry leaves on the ground scudded a few feet. Row on row of tiny waves, created by the wind, flowed up the pool's green surface. As quickly as it had come, the wind died, which left the clearing safe from the undead foulness once more. The heron stood in the shallows, motionless and waiting. Another little water snake swam up the pool, turning its periscope head from side to side.

Suddenly Lennie appeared out of the brush, and he came as silent as a creeping bear moves. The heron pounded the air with its wings, jacked itself clear of the water and flew off down river. The little snake slid in among the reeds at the pool's side, for any two-legged being were a threat. Lennie came quietly to the pool's edge. He knelt down and drank, barely touching his lips to the water, for he began to feel the fever of the Walking Plague. When a little bird skittered over the dry leaves behind him, his head jerked up and he strained toward the sound with eyes and ears until he saw the creature, and then he dropped his head and drank again.

When Lennie had finished, he sat down on the bank, with his side to the pool, so that he could watch the trail's entrance. He embraced his knees and laid his chin down on his knees. His head kept dipping and then jolting upright, trying to fend off fever induced slumber. The light climbed on out of the valley, and as it went, the tops of the mountains seemed to blaze with increasing brightness; this seemed worse to Lennie as his vision swam.

"I didn't forget, you bet, goddamn. Hide in the brush and wait for George," Lennie said softly to himself. He pulled his hat down low over his eyes to shield them from the light. He said, "George gonna give me hell. George gonna wish he was alone and not have me botherin' him."

Lennie was silent again, his mind fading in and out of consciousness. He turned his head and looked at the bright mountain tops.

"I can go right off there and find a cave," he said. Then he continued sadly, "and never have no ketchup … but I won't care. If George don't want me … I'll go away. I'll go away."

Then from out of Lennie's head, whether as a result of his broken mind or from the fever, there came the outside and alien presence in the form of a little fat old woman. She wore thick bull's-eye glasses and she wore a huge gingham apron with pockets, and she was starched and clean. She stood in front of Lennie and put her hands on her hips, and she frowned disapprovingly at him. Lennie recognised her as the woman who used to give him thumbs. Then, when she spoke, it was in Lennie's voice.

"I told you and told you," she said angrily. "I told you, 'Mind George 'cause he's such a nice fella and good to you.' But you don't never take no care. You do bad thin's."

Lennie answered her, "I tried and tried ma'am. I tried and tried. I couldn't help it."

"You never give a thought to George," she went on in Lennie's voice. "He been doin' nice thin's for you all the time. When he got a piece of pie you always got half or more than half. And if they was any Sick Ones tryna get you, he made sure they didn't."

"I know," said Lennie miserably. "I tried, ma'am. I tried and tried."

She loomed over him and interrupted, "All the time he coulda had such a good time if it wasn't for you. He woulda took his pay and raised hell in a whore house, and he coulda sit in a pool room and played snooker. Even gotta use twice as many bullets to keep you safe too! But he got to take care of you."

Lennie moaned with grief and said with fat tears rolling down his cheeks, "I know, ma'am. I'll go right off in the hills and I'll find a cave and I'll live there so I won't be no more trouble to George."

"You just say that," she said sharply. "You're always sayin' that, and you know son-of-a-bitchin' well you ain't never gonna do it. You'll just stick around and stew the b'Jesus outta George all the time."

Lennie said, "I might just as well go away. George ain't gonna let me tend no rabbits now."

"Well, maybe everyone would be better off if you became a Sick One!" she scoffed maliciously.

Then she was gone, and from out of Lennie's head there came a gigantic rabbit. It sat on its haunches in front of him, and it waggled its ears and crinkled its nose at him. Then it spoke in Lennie's voice too.

"Tend rabbits," it said scornfully. "You crazy bastard. You ain't fit to lick the boots of no rabbit. You'd forget them and let them go hungry. That's what you'd do. And then what would George think? You better off sick."

"I would not forget," Lennie said loudly.

"The hell you wouldn't," said the rabbit. "You ain't worth a greased jack-pin to ram you into hell. Christ knows George done everythin' he could to jack you outta the sewer, but it don't do no good. If you think George gonna let you tend rabbits, you're even crazier than usual. He ain't. He's gonna beat hell outta you with a stick, that's what he's gonna do. Gonna leave you to get eat!"

Now Lennie retorted belligerently, "He ain't neither. George won't do nothin' like that. I've knew George since ... I forget when ... and he ain't never raised his hand to me with a stick. He's nice to me. He ain't gonna be mean."

"Well, he's sick of you," said the rabbit. "He's gonna beat hell outta you and then go away and leave you."

"He won't," Lennie cried frantically. "He won't do nothin' like that. He won't let me get sick or get ate or beat me! I know George. Me and him travels together."

Then the rabbit repeated softly over and over, "He gonna leave you, you crazy bastard. He gonna leave you all alone. He gonna leave ya, crazy bastard."

Lennie put his hands over his ears and cried, "He ain't, I tell you he ain't. Oh! George! George! George!"

The rabbit laughed mockingly and said, "You wouldn't get beat if you just gave up and become a Sick One!"

George came quietly out of the brush and the rabbit scuttled back into Lennie's brain.

George said quietly, "What the hell you yellin' about?"

Lennie got up on his knees. "You ain't gonna leave me, are ya, George? I know you ain't."

George came stiffly near and sat down beside him.

"No," George finally said.

"I knew it. You ain't that kind," Lennie cried out happily. George was silent. Lennie then said, not quite a question but it was at the same time, "George."

"Yeah?" George sighed.

"I done another bad thin'," Lennie admitted.

"It don't make no difference," George said, and he fell silent again.

Only the topmost ridges were in the sun now. The shadow in the valley was blue and soft. From the distance came the sound of men shouting to one another. There was a gunshot, but not directed at them. George turned his head and listened to the commotion.

Lennie said, "George."

"Yeah?" George answered again.

"Ain't you gonna give me hell?" Lennie asked cautiously.

"Give you hell?" George asked, repeating the words back to him.

"Sure, like you always done before," Lennie replied excitedly. "Like, 'If I didn't have you I'd take my fifty bucks'—"

"Jesus Christ, Lennie! You can't remember nothin' that happens, but you remember every word I say," George shouted, cussing Lennie out.

"Well, ain't you gonna say it?" Lennie asked expectantly. George shook himself.

"If I was alone I could live so easy," he said woodenly. His voice was monotonous, and had no emphasis or inflexion. "I could get a job and not have no mess."

He stopped.

"Go on," said Lennie, almost pleading. "And when the enda the month come …"

"And when the end of the month came I could take my fifty bucks and go to a … cat house …" George said, trying to finish. He stopped again.

Lennie looked eagerly at him and said, "Go on, George. Ain't you gonna give me no more hell?"

"No," said George dejectedly.

"Well, I can go away," said Lennie, trying to bait George. "I'll go right off in the hills and find a cave if you don't want me."

George shook himself again, trying to hold himself together.

"No," he said. "I want you to stay with me here."

Lennie said craftily, "Tell me like you done before."

"Tell you what?" George said, trying not to look Lennie in the eye.

"About the other guys and about us," Lennie said, verbally prodding George.

George, repeating the speech he had rehearsed so many times before, said, "Guys like us got no family. They make a little stake and then they blow it in. They ain't got nobody in the world that gives a hoot in hell about them—"

"But not us. Tell about us now," Lennie cried happily. George was quiet for a moment. Then, when George hadn't responded, Lennie continued, "but not us. 'Cause—"

"'Cause I got you and—" George said, forcing the words out.

"And I got you. We got each other, that's what, that gives a hoot in hell about us!" Lennie cried in triumph, unable to wait for George to finish.

The little evening breeze blew over the clearing and the leaves rustled and the wind waves flowed up the green pool. Then the shouts of men sounded again, this time much closer than before.

George took off his hat and said shakily, "Take off your hat, Lennie. The air feels fine."

Lennie removed his hat dutifully and trustfully. He laid it on the ground in front of him. The shadow in the valley was bluer, and the evening came fast. On the wind, the sound of crashing in the brush came to them.

"Tell how it's gonna be," Lennie said dreamily. George had been listening to the distant sounds. The sound of people getting closer.

For a moment, George was business-like as he said, "Look across the river, Lennie, and I'll tell you so you can almost see it."

Lennie turned his head and looked off across the pool and up the darkening slopes of the Gabilan Mountains.

"We gonna get a little place," George began. He reached in his side pocket and brought out his Luger as well as Carlson's Luger. He snapped off the safety on both, and then let one hang loosely by his side. He looked at the back of Lennie's head, at the place where the spine and skull were joined. Lennie's collar and the back of his shirt was completely soaked through due to fever sweats. A man's voice called from up the river, and another man answered.

"Go on," said Lennie. George raised the gun and his hand shook, and then he dropped his hand to the ground again. Lennie's head dipped again, momentarily drifting out of consciousness and back in.

"We'll have … we'll have," George continued, struggling to maintain his composure.

"Go on," said Lennie with a tired smile. "How's it gonna be. We gonna get a little place."

"We'll have a cow," said George solemnly, "and we'll have maybe a pig and chickens … a big wall … and down the flat, we'll have a … little piece alfalfa—"

"For the rabbits!" Lennie shouted.

"For the rabbits," George repeated.

"And I get to tend the rabbits," Lennie reaffirmed.

"And you get to tend the rabbits," George confirmed.

Lennie giggled with happiness and said, without a care in the world, "And live offa fatta the lan'."

"Yes," George said without expression. Lennie tried to turn his head. George quickly said, interrupting Lennie's movement. "No, Lennie. Look down there across the river, like you can almost see the place."

Lennie obeyed him. George looked down at the gun. There were crashing footsteps in the brush now. George turned and looked toward them.

"Go on, George. When we gonna do it?" Lennie asked happily.

"We're gonna do it soon," George said stiffly.

"Me and you," Lennie nodded.

"You ... and me. Everybody gonna be nice to you. Ain't gonna be no more trouble. Nobody gonna hurt nobody nor steal from them," George said, struggling to not be choked by the lump in his throat.

"I thought you was mad at me, George," Lennie said beginning to slur his words.

"No," said George, shaking his head sadly. "No, Lennie. I ain't mad. I never been mad, and I ain't now. That's a thin' I want you to know."

The voices came close now. George raised the gun again and listened to the voices.

Lennie begged, "Let's ... do it now. Let's get that place ... now."

"Sure, right now. I gotta ... we gotta," George said with a nod. Then George raised the gun and steadied it, and he brought the muzzle of it close to the base of Lennie's head, careful to not put the cold muzzle to Lennie's skin. George considered if someone with the Walking Plague was even themselves after they'd become a walking corpse. Were they still in there somewhere? Was an existence as a Sick One better than death? *No.* It couldn't be. To even turn and give into the Walking Plague was terrible. George's hand shook violently, but his face set and his hand steadied. He pulled the trigger. The crash of the shot rolled up the hills and rolled down again. Lennie jarred, then settled slowly forward to the sand, and he lay without quivering. George shivered and looked at the gun, but he wasn't done. He threw Carlson's Luger down by Lennie and held his own gun. The brush seemed filled with cries and with the sound of running feet.

Slim's voice shouted, "George. Where you at, George?"

But George sat stiffly on the bank and looked at his right hand that had thrown the gun away. The group burst into the clearing, and Curley was at the forefront. He saw Lennie lying on the sand.

"Got him, by God," Curley said with a smile. He went over and looked down at Lennie, and then he looked back at George. He said softly, "Right in the back of the head."

Slim came directly to George and sat down beside him, sat very close to him.

"Never you mind," Slim whispered to George. "A guy got to sometimes."

But Carlson was standing over George and asked, "How'd you do it?"

"I just done it," George said with exhaustion – he was so tired.

"Did he have my gun?" Carlson said looking around.

"Yeah. He had your gun," George sighed, nodding to the Luger.

"And you got it away from him before he shot you?" Carlson asked, staring at George.

"Yeah. That's how," George said, his voice was almost a whisper. He looked steadily at his left hand that had held the gun.

Slim twitched George's elbow and said softly, "Come on, George. Me and you'll go and get a drink."

George let himself be helped to his feet and repeated, "Yeah, a drink."

Slim said simply, "You had to, George. I swear you had to. Come on with me."

He led George into the entrance of the trail and up toward the highway. Curley and Carlson looked after them.

Finally, Carlson said, "Now what the hell you suppose is eatin' them two guys?"

"I don't know," Curley replied, moping the sweat from his forehead. "But ... I think I got a fever comin'."

ABOUT THE AUTHOR

I always enjoyed reading fictional worlds, but creating my own was always my passion. My Year 8 English teacher told me I should pursue writing after a short story I had written for a school project.

Things changed and life moved on, but even while I was graduating from my Bachelors and Masters in Psychology, I still wrote stories and I still loved doing it. Writing is my passion, and everything else I do is a means for me to carry on with that passion.

I'm also prepared to move to a secure location at a zombie's notice …

If you've gotten this far, please leave me a review and message me; I love hearing what people think!

For my website:

www.AmongTheDead.co.uk

For regular updates:

www.facebook.com/AmongTheDeadATD

www.twitter.com/AmongTheDeadATD.

Want to email me?

AmongTheDeadATD@hotmail.com

Printed in Poland
by Amazon Fulfillment
Poland Sp. z o.o., Wrocław

49663801R00082